EVERY SIN~~GLE~~

Úna =
Nuala o'fdoolain

Noeleen =
Nell M'Cafferty

Also by Hugo Hamilton

Surrogate City
The Last Shot
The Love Test
Dublin Where the Palm Trees Grow
Headbanger
Sad Bastard
The Speckled People
The Sailor in the Wardrobe
Disguise
Hand in the Fire

HUGO HAMILTON

Every Single Minute

FOURTH ESTATE • *London*

First published in Great Britain in 2014 by
Fourth Estate
An imprint of HarperCollins*Publishers*
77–85 Fulham Palace Road,
Hammersmith, London W6 8JB
www.4thestate.co.uk

1

A catalogue record for this book is available from the British Library.

ISBN 978-0-00-732485-9

Typeset by Palimpsest Book Production Ltd, Falkirk, Stirlingshire
Printed and bound in Great Britain by Clays Ltd, St Ives plc

MIX
Paper from
responsible sources
FSC
www.fsc.org
FSC® C007454

For Mary Rose

Where can I find another brother, ever?

Sophocles/Seamus Heaney

1

She's wearing those red canvas shoes. They're in all the photographs. They're there at the airport, while she's being helped down the steps. They're there in the Botanic Garden. At the Pergamon Museum. Also outside the opera house. They made her feel light on her feet. You know them, those flat canvas shoes with the white rubber soles and white rubber toe-caps and rough white stitching. Sneakers, people sometimes call them. Converse, if you prefer, with two rows of steel eyelets punched into the canvas for the laces, white laces. And two extra eyelets on each side for no other reason than to make them look more sporty, I suppose, more industrial maybe.

They're there at the hotel, beside her bed. She's sitting in her chair, ready to go out. She's got white socks on, from some long-haul flight, I think, and I'm helping her on with the shoes, the red canvas shoes. I get the laces done up and help her onto her feet. I've double-parked the wheelchair next to her chair so I can swing her around, holding her by the elbows and letting her down slowly. I can hear her breathing.

Will she be warm enough? By right she should have some kind of scarf to put on because her neck is quite exposed. She says she'll be fine, she can always hold the collar of her coat up.

She wanted to be brought to Berlin. I was bringing her. She loved travelling and it was her last wish to go somewhere away. Anywhere, she said. Anywhere away. So why not Berlin, I suggested, and she said yes, why not? Berlin was one of those places she had always been putting off and now she was afraid she might never see the city in her own lifetime. I love the way they do potatoes in Germany, she said. I want to see the Pergamon Museum. I want to see the Botanic Garden. I want to see the church that's been left in ruins since the war.

This is different, she said to me a couple of times on the flight coming over from Dublin. She was actually crying in that photograph, taken by the flight attendant. She was crying and smiling at the same time, saying this is different, Liam. This is different.

I think she might have been afraid of what the photograph was doing to her. It was keeping her. It was keeping her and it was leaving her behind.

She kept saying it was different because there was a bit of travelling left in her and going to Berlin was giving her something to live for. It was like extra time, if you can call it that. There's nothing wrong with me only I'm dying, she said. I suppose she was trying to laugh it off sometimes, doing her best to ignore the reality, you can understand that. She had all this energy, she wanted to see everything. All the galleries. All the museums, all the gardens, all the places unvisited before, the history, the whole place changing after the Berlin Wall, the way the city looks here and now, alive and breathing and remembering, everything we can humanly fit in, she said. She had a list made out, written on hotel paper, the itinerary, if you like.

I won't forget this, she said to me.

She said she loved every single minute. She said she would remember this journey as long as she lived. I know that doesn't make sense under the circumstances, but you know what she was getting at. What people say is not always word for word. She said a lot of hopeful things about the world and the future, because it's hard to get out of the habit of looking forward and being optimistic. It's hard to stop saying as long as you live, even though you can never tell how long that's going to be for.

She only had a bit over a week after that.

She asked me to book tickets for the opera. She wanted to go to the Berlin State Opera, it's not far from the Adlon where we were staying. *Don Carlo* was running at the time.

Verdi, she said. We have to go. The last time I saw *Don Carlo* was at the Met, in New York.

Unfortunately the performance was sold out. I called the reception at the hotel to see if there was any chance of them getting tickets for us. They were extremely helpful. They did say it was a bit late in the day, but they assured me they would do their very best and if there was a spare ticket to be found anywhere in Berlin it was hers.

I told her it was looking good.

Thanks, Liam, she said.

And then she pulls off the wig that she's wearing. A full head of hair, with light brown curls, not unlike her own. She pulls it off with both hands like a child and throws it across the room as if she never found anything she hated as much. In fact, the first time she put the wig on she had to laugh. As if she was only pretending to be grown up, wearing something belonging to the adults, don't I look very funny in this? You wouldn't recognize her in those photographs if you didn't know her. She looks so unlike herself without the curly hair, so uncovered. Her face is a bit puffed up with medication, swollen around the eyes. I think the real reason for the wig was so as not to frighten people, because she could see the shock in their eyes when they saw her head bare, how quickly this can happen to anyone.

I'm not wearing that thing, she says.

I don't blame you.

I want to be myself, she says.

The wig is left lying on the floor like an animal that's been run over on the motorway. I pick it up and carry it away, back to her suitcase.

Then I take off my cap and give it to her, because she can't be going out with nothing covering her head. This is Berlin in May we're talking about. We can't be sure if it's going to be warm or cold.

Here, why don't you wear my cap?

4

What I have is a grey baseball-type cap, pretty ordinary, no brand name on it. She examines the cap in her hands for a moment. She makes no comment, she doesn't look at herself in the mirror, she doesn't trust mirrors. The cap fits her and I'm hoping she will keep it on, she looks great. I tell her it goes with the shoes, the red canvas shoes.

Now you look like Steven Spielberg.

She laughs.

Sure what does it matter? she says. I'm here in Berlin, nobody can see me.

And the way she said things like that you'd never forget. You'd recognize her anywhere by the way she spoke in a high voice, quite innocent, as if everything was new to her. Her voice was a girl. Her mind was a girl. She loved everything she didn't know yet. She loved the whole idea of letting on that she knew nothing so that people would explain things to her very clearly, in simple words, and she would not be expected to say anything. She would tilt her head and listen carefully and wait for them to tell her things they might never say to a grown-up woman, or a man.

Nobody sees a child watching, she said.

Some of the things she said, I have to admit, didn't make sense to me until after she died. While she was still alive I may have been prevented from understanding a lot of what she was saying until now, looking back. I know this sounds like a contradiction, but it's hard sometimes to see exactly what's in front of you until you get around to remembering. I hope this is accurate. I hope I'm getting it all in the right order. I'm only going by the photographs and the places we went to see. And what she said at the time might not be the same as what I remember she said.

2

The bag she had. She had this see-through plastic bag with a white zip across the top. I think it might have come with a pillow, or a duvet cover, something like that. It was a heavy-duty bag with proper white rope handles, completely clear with no product name, so you could see all the contents inside. Everything she had with her, all her belongings, if you like. From the outside you could see her purse, her medication, her tissues, her reading glasses, her passport, the key card for the hotel room, bits of newspapers she was keeping for later. A book she was never going to read. Her mobile phone, switched off. Things taken from the hotel room like free pens.

And chocolate. Lots of chocolate.

What are we only children? That's what she said to me.

Not that she was stuck for a bag. She could have got herself any bag she wanted, only handbags were never a great priority in her life. That see-through bag was perfectly good, she said, too good to be thrown out. She held on to it for environmental reasons, obviously, but also to let people know that she was not the kind of woman who would spend a lot of money on a designer bag, that's not who she was. She wasn't here to make a big impression, it was only a bag to put her things into. I think she was making the point that her life was very open, nothing to hide. It could only have been her bag and nobody else's, unmistakable. And it was handy being able to see into the bag from the outside while searching with her hand inside at the same time. Her hand became one of the items in the bag and the plastic made a squeaking sound while she was looking for something, her glasses, checking to make sure she had her glasses, with the wine-coloured frames. She had only recently bought them in New York and she told me that the optometrist had nice breath. She tried to get him into conversation, but all he ever said was look up, look down at the floor, look at my left ear. And the same thing again for the other eye, look up, look down, look at my right ear. He was so close in front of her that she got the smell of blackberries on his breath, like blackberry jam.

We're only children. That's it. We're only just children, she said.

She liked to imagine that every day was the first day of her life. She loved being at the Adlon, a bit of luxury, she said. The foyer was wide, with a section cordoned off at the centre for tables and chairs where people sat having coffee and cake, a glass of champagne, like they had done for years, I suppose. There was a high dome lit up in the middle of the ceiling and a balcony overlooking the foyer where people could look down from above at the people below. The reception was to the left as you came in, that's how I remember it, and a cocktail bar to the right. And there was a long marble corridor leading away to the back past the elevators. It was a calm place, all in all, even when it was busy, with a piano playing most of the time and voices chatting and the sound of the elevator doors. She loved meeting new people, for example the hotel staff. She got into conversation and made friends with them right away, asking them questions, personal questions like do you believe in ghosts? Do you have a boyfriend? What do you think of Lady Gaga? And they always responded truthfully, out of courtesy. She talked to them like she was one of the hotel staff herself, which she was once, long ago, in London, a chambermaid, if that's what you still call room service now. She was like one of them, having a chat to fill in the time, keeping them from their work.

Her room was bigger, more deluxe than mine, overlooking the street with all the action. My room looked out over the inner courtyard with the flower garden. There was possibly a bit too much décor, if you ask me, needless use of natural resources. Wood panelling around the rooms, all very heavy and executive. Corporate, would that be the right word? And the bathrooms were something else, very spacious, marble tiling, beautiful towels that looked to me like they had never been used before, that was the feeling you got at least. Everything was very new and old-looking at the same time, new old. The place had been completely reconstructed since the wall came down, with no trace of the old place left, only the name and the reputation.

Sometimes I wonder what people get up to in hotel bedrooms, what mad things went on before me. It doesn't bear thinking about, she said. Leave it alone, you don't want to imagine. Because she worked as a chambermaid in London years ago and she'd seen everything that was worth imagining. It was her job to erase the evidence. A hotel bedroom is meant to have no trace of the previous occupants. Maybe all they ever get up to is look into each other's eyes and say each other's names, out loud.

So we're all ready to go and she takes out the list from her bag. I'm pushing the wheelchair along the corridor towards the elevator. I call the elevator and she hands me the list to give to the driver when we see him.

We're not going to call him the driver, she says. Are we?

We can call him Manfred.

Does he mind being called Manfred?

That's his name, I tell her. Please call me Manfred, that's what he said to me.

She wants to know, does he have much English? Yes.

Don't tell him, she says, will you?

She would prefer Manfred not to know about her condition. It's not like her to withhold information from people, but keeping Manfred free from knowing that she is dying is not such a big lie, everybody does that.

She would rather not have to explain. She probably doesn't want to go over those medical details again. What the doctors said, how they waved the X-ray around and then left her alone in the corridor. How they came back and told her that in spite of the bad news, she was as healthy as a trout. Her heart was in excellent condition, and her blood pressure was perfect. They were talking about her like spare body parts, she told me, as though they could reassemble the best available parts from a number of women into one decent woman they could stand over. The nurse even remarked about her elbows, how did she keep them so young, she had the elbows of a ten-year-old.

I've let him know you're a writer, I tell her.

He doesn't need to know any more than that, she says.

He thinks you're my mother.

She laughs at that. Me, your mother?

Everybody loves mothers, I say, and she laughs again, with all her lungs.

I wouldn't know how to be a mother, she says.

Ah that's not true.

She's not my mother, only Manfred has picked up that impression somehow because she's a good bit older than me, in a wheelchair.

Just to be clear about this, she was definitely not my mother and there was no romance between us either, nothing like that in the past, no previous history. We were not attached to each other or living together like lovers, or married, or related in any compulsory way, like her family. We were good

11

friends, that's all. We met when things were a bit upside-down, for both of us. She was older in years, in books, in everything. She didn't mind me knowing less than she did. She didn't mind not knowing the first thing about cooking, I wouldn't let her near a kitchen. We clicked, I suppose, just telling each other things, having a laugh. We took each other seriously, but not all the time. I used to call around to play with her dog, Buddy, throwing her shoe across the room to make him go after it, while she was reading. She had the ability to read as if there was nobody else in the world outside the book. Even with me running around her chair and Buddy after me, she would continue reading, even when I was hiding the shoe behind her back so that Buddy would have to jump right across her and the book would go flying out of her hands, only then she would look up and say, Liam, I'm going to kill you.

Manfred is waiting at the reception by the time we get down. As we come out of the elevator he is walking towards us and I get the impression that he has been walking towards us for some time, maybe hours, maybe days, maybe always was walking towards us. How did he know when to start walking, I'm asking myself. He's got a shaved head and you wouldn't say he's overweight, just very big all round, in a physical sense, he does weights, it's obvious. He's wearing a suit and tie and his chest is expanding to an enormous size as he puts out his hand, smiling. The piano is playing somewhere, up at the balcony level, I think it was.

I give Manfred the itinerary and tell him that we

12

can always change the order as we go along, and we're open to anything else of interest that's not already included on the list, if there's enough time left. He looks at the list for a moment as though we might have the wrong city. She has everything listed all over the place, the way it happened in history. He points with his finger, blowing out air through his lips, lining the places up in some kind of order that would make sense to him geographically, as a driver.

And while I'm talking to Manfred, she's looking back at the elevator we have just come from, staring at the old-fashioned dial above the doors, maybe wondering if that's how Manfred guessed we were on our way down. It's one of the features of the old Adlon which they have reinstated in the new Adlon. Like in the Hitchcock films. A dial pointing to the different levels like a clock, letting you know where the elevator is, in case you want to know.

Here, let me take your mother, Manfred says.

He grabs the handles of the wheelchair out of my hands and away she goes, wearing her cap and her red canvas shoes, holding the clear, see-through bag with all her belongings, nothing hidden. Down the marble wheelchair ramp at the side, through the automatic doors, out under the red canopy towards the tour buses waiting in the street. Manfred pushes her over to the car and opens the sliding door. And after she's got into the car I discover that the sliding door closes electronically. Please leave it alone, Manfred says to me when I try to close it myself, manually.

In the square in front of the Brandenburg Gate there is some kind of demonstration going on. A small gathering of people with placards, more policemen than demonstrators. It's all very calm, a lot of chanting, I think it's for Tibet.

And Manfred is right, absolutely, she was like a mother. She gave advice like a mother, she asked questions like a mother, she bossed people around like a mother. You can't have cake for your main meal, with beer. Eat something decent, Liam, look at you, the vultures would pass over you. That kind of thing she would say. As if she was responsible for me. But she would let you have anything you want after all, you could always get around her, and she insisted on paying for everything. She had a mother's way of stepping into your life and giving a running commentary on everything that was going on, telling you what you were doing right or wrong while you were doing it. She cross-examined you like a mother, holding your arm and looking inside your head and saying out loud all the things you were keeping to yourself. She could guess what you were thinking. No wonder everyone thought she was my mother. She was like a mother to everyone. Indiscriminately. Even Manfred, the driver, she held his arm while he was helping her into the car, asking him questions until he told her that he was half-Turkish on his mother's side and married with three children under ten. She said she was a hundred percent Irish and she would love to be half something else.

Maybe that's what happens when you have no

14

children of your own, you turn everyone else into children. She even spoke like a mother about Tibet.

God love them, she said, they only want to be themselves.

3

So we're sitting side by side in the back of a large grey-coloured car and she's telling me about the opera, *Don Carlo*. She's saying it's basically a big family story, not unlike her own. The conversation we have is quite random initially. She's wondering about her dog. Will Buddy be all right, Liam, do you think? Yes, he's perfectly happy, I assure her. She tells me to remind her about the sheets. The sheets, Liam, don't let me forget the sheets. Because she has everything planned out in advance and it's her intention to buy a new pair of sheets in Berlin to bring home with her to Dublin.

Manfred is taking us through the big park, past the golden angel, it's been seen in lots of movies, and music videos. The day is sunny and there are people out walking with take-away coffees. Running with bottles of water. And dogs. Running with dogs. Cycling with dogs. Look at that, she says, pointing to a man cycling with a child inside a trailer cart attached to the back of his bicycle. Or is it two children? That's not something you see

16

very much of in Dublin, she says. She talks about the amount of women on bicycles without helmets. Right out in the middle of the traffic. She says you wouldn't find her cycling without a helmet in any city now. We come out of the park and pass by a large yellow brick building in a modern design that looks like a pirate's hat, she says. It's the Berlin Philharmonic. Another place she would love to include on the list.

Then she tells me why she loves *Don Carlo*.

The plot is a bit complicated, from what I remember. It's about a father killing his own son. The King is forced to hand over his son in order to keep his reign, that's the outline in a simple sentence. It's set in Spain during the Spanish Inquisition. The King is trying to bring order to the world by force and his son Don Carlos is against all that brutality, he wants to stop the killing and everyone to go home and live in peace with the person they love. Power is all that matters to the King. He's addicted to power and he's got to do everything to keep it, including killing his own son. It's a terrible decision he has to make and he's full of guilt and remorse, going against all his instincts as a father. There is an added problem. The son, Don Carlos, is in love with a French woman, but his father has already married her by force and made her the Queen. She still loves Don Carlos and Don Carlos is heartbroken. That gives his father a further reason for mistrusting his son and getting him out of the way. I know it sounds a bit simplistic, but that's it, more or less, a big family drama.

He must kill the love within himself, she says. The

17

King has to kill the love inside in order to kill his own son.

The opera keeps reminding her of her own family, that's why she's so keen on seeing it again. It's the story of every family, she tells me. That's why *Don Carlo* has remained so popular over the years, because we can all read our own lives into the story, it's universal. Every time she goes to see it she cannot help thinking of her own father and what happened to her brother, her little brother. It's the power of the drama that makes you think it's your own story which is being portrayed on stage, she says, you become part of what's happening right in front of your eyes. She says her imagination is too big. She's like a girl again, watching the story of her family unfolding around her. She's so taken by the opera each time that she can see her brother coming back to life on stage. Her father killing the love inside himself. Her brother being taken away in the end. And she's completely helpless, trapped in her seat, listening to the music. There's nothing she can do to intervene.

We used to go to the theatre together, the odd time in Dublin. She would be given complimentary tickets and ask me to go with her, as a companion. We would have an early meal somewhere and get to the theatre with time to spare so she could meet people. You could see them nudging each other, the lips moving. She would disappear into the crowd, pulled along by one handshake after another, passed on from one group to the next, until she needed to escape. Just when they were beginning to tell her something about herself that she already knew, she would point to me standing at the bar and tell them that she had somebody waiting for her. All these theatregoers she knew, I wouldn't have a clue who they were, other writers, journalists, TV personalities, faces that everybody knows. What I remember most is people coming up to her at the interval saying they had read her book. And she would hunch up with all that praise, like a light was hurting her eyes. A woman once turned around and stood right up in her seat and reached back across two rows to shake her hand and say thank you. That's all the woman said to her, thanks, for being so honest, for being herself, for writing the story of her life and her family without hiding anything.

It was mostly families we talked about in Berlin. We talked about *Don Carlo* and fathers and mothers and brothers. We talked about men and women and aunts and uncles and children and Jesuits and love and weddings and life and friends and lovers, the whole lot, I suppose. The things that happen in families. Which includes almost everything, doesn't it? We were going around the city looking at the sights and telling each other these stories. Family stories and love stories come right and wrong, she said.

Is love still a good word for love, she asked me at one point. I mean, how can you answer that? Of course it's still a good word. It's the best word there is for love. What other word is there that would work any better? Chemistry? She said they were always making young words out of the old words, changing the meaning so you don't recognize them any more. And love is one of those words like home and hope and passion, all those words that people never put back in the right place, she said.

I think being away in Berlin allowed us both to be quite open with each other. It helped us to forget what was happening to her, it was all on hold. There was a comfort in not having to think about what was imminent, I suppose. As long as we kept moving and telling each other stories, as long as the streets were going by and we had all these family things to talk about. I think it was not having to explain anything that made it easier to explain everything, if you get me.

4

She's on a lot of steroids to help with her breathing. She's searching in her see-through bag and takes out some medication. She reads the label and drops it back into the bag. She holds up the bag and looks inside. Because it's easier to find things like that from the outside. She reaches in with her hand once more and takes out other medication, then looks at the label and drops that back into the bag also. It's hard to know if she's picking out the same one each time or if they're always different.

She said your life is a pair of lungs. Time is a pair of lungs. Could that be right? You're only as good as your lungs and her lungs had run out of time, something like that she said.

She described to me what it's like going into hospital for a breathing test. The nurse gets you to sit down in front of a machine called the pulmonary function test. You put your lips around a nozzle that looks like a gum shield attached to the machine, then the nurse tells you to take in a deep breath until your lungs are completely full up and you hold it for as long as possible. Then you blow all the way out until your lungs are completely empty. And when you're ready, she said the nurse says it all like a breathing song. Take in a deep breath, all the way in, right up to the top of your lungs and hold it, hold it, hold it, she says, hold it, hold it, very good, now blast all the way out, all the way, all the way, keep going, she says, all the way, all the way, all the way, keep going, every last bit, very good, excellent, well done, she says, until your face has gone all red from the effort and the nurse tells you to relax and breathe in normally and let's try that again, one more time.

As well as the steroids, she's also taking pain-killers. And they've given her Xanax, too, so she can relax and sleep at night.

At the hotel she told me that she was afraid some-times. I'm afraid of drowning, she said. I'm afraid my lungs will fill up and then I'll drown. That's what happens, you know, when you get pneumonia, it's like drowning. I'm afraid of drowning alone, she said. The Xanax was meant to stop all that anxiety. She said it makes you more like yourself, back to the way you were before, the real your-self. Because she was worried, naturally, and she found it difficult to concentrate. Apart from a few articles in the newspapers, I think she had trouble absorbing too much news. She was more interested in seeing things first-hand now, listening to people. She couldn't write. She didn't see the point in putting things down any more. She had no time for things that were made up, she couldn't read a novel or watch a movie, for example, there was no time for anything invented.

Only *Don Carlo*, because it was so personal to her.

She offers me a Xanax in the car, as if I need it. She starts laughing and shaking her see-through plastic bag around. Like she's offering around mints or chocolate. Here, would anybody like a Xanax? Manfred ignores her. He's in his own world and remains focused on the driving. Anyway it's not something that should be given to a person operating machinery. I don't need one either, but she says it will do me no harm, why not? So I take one for a laugh, see if it does anything for me.

I tell her that my daughter, Maeve, is getting married.

That's great news, Liam.

She thinks I'm obsessed with my daughter. She doesn't like me going on too much about Maeve all the time, I can understand that, because she has no children herself and this whole father and daughter thing gets to her a bit. I think it makes her feel excluded. She usually tells me to shut up. So I give her the details in brief, the wedding is planned for August.

That's very soon, she says.

You'll be getting an invitation, I tell her.

Thanks, she says.

And then I realize what I've just said. There's not a hope in hell of her being able to attend the wedding. Maybe it's the Xanax. It must be making me feel more like myself.

I'm coming, she says.

But it's three months away.

I'll be there, Liam. Whether I'm dead or alive. Where are they having it?

It seems like the future has abandoned her, all these things carrying on in her absence.

The wedding, Liam? Where are they having it?

On the farm, I tell her, his farm, Shane. It's his mother and father, they're very keen to have a wedding on the farm. They have these great barns and the ruins of an old church on their land. They want to have the wedding in the old ruins and then I suppose they're intending to get a marquee, just in case of the weather. It's a fully working farm, with live cattle and so forth. But knowing Shane, he will get that all fixed up, taking into account the wedding guests and their clothes and shoes, I would imagine. At least, that is what they're talking about.

A farm wedding, she says. I would love to be there.

She once showed me a photograph of herself when she was the same age as Maeve. No more than twenty-four years old, twenty-five at the most. With lots of curls. It was taken before she went to London, before she worked as a chambermaid, when she was getting out, leaving her family and her country behind. With no fear and no idea what was coming. I wish I had met her then, the life in her. She must have been great fun in that photograph, full of danger and up for anything, all kinds of things not even thought up yet. The look in her eyes. Staring right at you. I think it was the eyebrows you noticed most. Striking, you would have to say, drawn by a child. Her eyes look like they had great questions to ask.

She has the same eyes in Berlin. They are the eyes of a twenty-four-year-old girl, with the eyebrows left intact, even though all her hair is gone from radiation and her lungs are working very hard and she can't get enough air to say all the things she still wants to tell me.

She talks about a place she once went to which was great for the lungs. The salt mine she went to visit in Romania, in Transylvania. It was an active salt mine, fully operational, but all the people with bad lungs came there because the salt dried the air for them. That's when she was travelling with Noleen. Herself and Noleen, they travelled all the way down from the Ukrainian border, right down to Tirana and back around the coast to Italy.

Lots of people told them to go to the salt mine. Patients with pulmonary trouble came from all over the country, all over the world in fact. People even asked them where they were from, as if they had come especially for their lungs, all the way from Ireland. She told them she had lungs like a damp cottage and they said she had come to the right place. It's a famous mine, she says, like a place of pilgrimage without prayers, with the same air temperature day and night. She describes the trucks carrying out boulders of stone-white salt, and the people coming to inhale and straighten out their shoulders. Lots of people in wheelchairs. Grandmothers and all. Even people who were off the cigarettes having a cigarette, why not? Because the air was so clear it was crackling in your nostrils, she says. Whole families going for a picnic down there with fold-up chairs and a portable cassette player making hardly any noise because the place was so big. All the children breathing up and down and playing football in a huge underground stadium, she says. With floodlights. And goal posts marked out on the salt walls.

And after the salt mine, she's telling me, they went swimming nearby in a salt lake that never freezes. It was the strangest feeling, she says. Floating on top of the water. Their legs were rising up out of the lake in front of them like buoyancy bags, you couldn't keep them down. That's what happens, your legs feel weightless, she says. And Noleen had a way of turning everything that went wrong into something to laugh at. When they were coming out of the lake they must have chosen a spot that was very muddy, because they were covered in mud like female wrestlers, the two of them laughing and holding on to each other, hardly able to stand up.

Travelling unlimited, she says.

She says her lungs are left in Romania. My lungs are in Romania, she says, and my head is in New York and my feet are in Berlin and the rest of me is in Dublin.

5

I heard her speaking a number of times in public. I saw her on stage once at the literary festival in Ennis, County Clare, in the Old Ground Hotel. I also saw her in Colorado, in Aspen. It was my first time in the Rocky Mountains, but they were very familiar to me already. I had a good memory of those mountains from watching television as a boy. I had also heard a lot of songs that were written about that part of America.

Some of the things she said in Ennis she also said in Aspen. She was there to speak about herself and her family. What life was like for a Dublin woman in her own time. How things have changed and how much better things are now and how much has gone missing. She was well known for speaking straight from the heart, no matter where she was, Ennis or Aspen. She was the world expert on her own childhood and what happened inside her family, nobody could argue with her about those facts. People everywhere in Ennis and Aspen loved hearing what things were like in Ireland and why she could never forgive her mother and father.

The problem was that every time she spoke in public, she would get herself worked up, she got angry, she cried openly. People wanted to hear everything in person nowadays and that left her vulnerable, stepping back into her own childhood and remembering it all over again as if it happened only recently and it was never going to be over. Every time she spoke about these things in public she had to back them up emotionally, in tears, as if nobody would believe her unless she cried.

Sometimes I was afraid the story was getting magnified each time she told it. You know the way you remember things larger than they actually were, whenever you speak about them, just because somebody is good enough to listen. People in the audience were so enthusiastic, she may have been forced to make things look worse. Or maybe it was just a matter of finding the best words to describe the worst things. She had a good memory for bad memory, so she said herself.

Or does everything get smaller when you talk about it?

My concern at the time was her not being able to let go. I hated seeing her crying in public. It was hard to watch her taking out a handkerchief from her sleeve, or not even doing that, allowing herself to cry openly without any attempt to hide her tears. So I made a suggestion to her, as a friend, in good faith. I think it was being away in Aspen that made me say things I would never have thought of in

Ennis. The mountains allowed me to put forward the idea that she might try to understand her mother and father a bit more. Not that she would have to forgive them or anything like that, I was not questioning her story or saying it didn't happen, only that sometimes when she spoke, it took too much out of her. Why not try and put it behind you?

For your own peace of mind.

I was saying this because I had the same problem with my own father following me all the time, even though he's dead now. The fact is, he never goes away and I'm still afraid of his anger. Sometimes I think it might be better to pretend you never had a father, even for a while now and again, like a short vacation from your memory, instead of sitting up all night like a child waiting for him.

She listened to me. She tilted her head as usual and allowed me to speak my mind. I thought I was doing quite well, making some good points that were worth considering at least. I was only saying that remembering your childhood is not all that it's made out to be. And you need to give your father the right to reply, especially if he's not around to speak up for himself. Otherwise it's like a military tribunal. That's all I'm saying, you need to step into their shoes and see their point of view.

That's rubbish, Liam.

She said the altitude was beginning to affect me. I was not thinking properly. The clouds were below the hotel and the air was so thin, oxygen-depleted, my understanding of things had become a bit simplistic.

It's my life, she said.

I'm only trying to help you get over it, I said.

You want me to abandon my brother?

She was having a yoghurt, I remember. In her room, overlooking the mountains. She was telling me that her memory was all she had to go by. Your memory keeps changing and you have to keep up with it, she said. The yoghurt was finished but she was still finding tiny bits. She picked up the tin-foil lid and licked the remaining yoghurt off until it was shining and then she went back to the carton again.

She said that's what writers do, they search around for things to write about in their memory, like a human laboratory. It's not really possible to make things up out of nothing, she said. Nothing is invented, only things that have already happened in some way or another happening all over again in your imagination in more and more fantastic ways.

She continued going around the yoghurt carton with the spoon, so I got the impression she was looking for something in it to write about.

You're not going to find anything more in there, I said.

She stared at me. You never knew how she was going to take something like that, she might laugh with you or she might go the other way.

You're living in a fantasy, Liam. That's what she said to me. You think it's possible to walk around with no memory. You think it's humanly possible to put everything behind you and walk away like you're leaving behind an empty field, or an empty barn?

Ah Jaysus, Úna. I'm only saying, give your parents a break, you can't blame them for everything.

Well you should have heard her. She accused me of trying to take her childhood away from her, stealing everything she had to write about. I could hear the emotion rising in her voice, as if she couldn't speak the words fast enough. I can't even remember half of what she said, all about children being kept quiet by letting them put their hand in a jar of satin sweets so they wouldn't listen to what the adults were saying. She said I was trying to claim that she was a child invisible, with no interest in the world.

You're just like the rest of them, she said. You want me to keep my mouth shut, don't you? You want me to pretend I never heard what happened to women inside their own homes. You think I just went to school peacefully with the nuns and slept with my hands crossed over my chest.

For God's sake, Úna.

You think I'm just putting on an Irish accent and letting on that I'm from Dublin, is that it?

The conversation started to escalate, out of my hands. She made it look like I had never been a child myself. Like I had said something unforgivable against all children, all women.

I'm not stealing anything from you, I said.

You think I never saw the bloody sawdust on the floor of the butchers?

I'm not disputing your childhood, I said.

You're being cruel to me, Liam.

Look, Úna. I'm on your side, one hundred percent. I just don't want you to be a victim.

A victim, she said.

That was it. She gave me a filthy look.

A victim? She repeated the word a number of times, speaking towards the door as if she was addressing somebody else, like there was an audience in the room and she was asking them to agree with her, getting them to say that I had no compassion. What I was implying was so wrong, so hurtful, so insensitive, not even allowing her to be a victim. She turned on me with her eyes and said that was exactly what happened to victims of all crimes, they were made to feel responsible for the injustice that was done to them.

I'm not saying that, Úna.

That's what being a victim is, Liam, you feel it's your own fault.

Let go the injustice, that's all I'm saying.

We don't have the right to let go, she said. How are we going to change anything if we don't remember?

I don't want to be a victim, I said.

You think you have a choice, Liam? Is that it? You think people can just decide whether they want to be a victim or not? It's just a lifestyle thing, is that what you're saying? Look at you. You haven't come out all that well either, have you? Just take a look at yourself, Liam. You're a mess. That's what you are.

A mess.

She knew that was out of order. I was waiting for her to put it right, to say that everybody was a mess, not just me, all of us, herself included, but she said nothing and neither did I. She put her finger into the yoghurt carton and began twirling it around. Then she licked her finger and looked straight out the window at the mountains.

I walked out. I didn't even care if we remained friends after that. I was having nothing more to do with her. I couldn't be arsed to go and listen to her speaking in public, but then she phoned me to apologize.

Liam, I'm really sorry, she said.

She said I was not a mess. She said I was anything but a mess and I was absolutely right about everything.

I'm full of self-pity sometimes, she said. I don't know why I'm like this. I keep losing all my friends. That's why nobody likes me, she said, I'm so obsessed with myself. I can only remember what was done to me. Please, Liam, I'm sorry. You're the only friend I have left.

Which was not strictly true, she had friends everywhere. But we made up, sort of. You know the way it is, you take a person good and bad. Like she was taking me good and bad. We were good and bad together, you could say.

I went to see her on stage after all, in front of a massive audience. This is Aspen, not Ennis, we're talking about, so they came from all over America to listen to her. And you know what, nothing changed, she said the same things all over again, word for word. She spoke even more forcefully, like she had only been rehearsing it with me in her room. She spoke like a woman who had never been given

33

a chance to speak before and she was going to leave nothing unsaid this time. It felt as though she was looking straight at me and I was left with no right to reply. You could hear her inhaling. You could hear her mouth clicking. She said the loneliest person in the world was the person who could not tell their own story. And that's how it was for her before she began to write her memoir. She said you become locked into your own silence and it's like not being alive at all any more. Until you write the story down and claim your own life back and stop being at the mercy of what happened to you.

I was at the mercy, she said.

She spoke about *Don Carlo*. She said she had seen it lately at the Met in New York. It was fabulous, she said. It was like the story of her own family. She said her father was just like the King, obsessed with his own power and his own fame around Dublin. Her father had no love for his son. Her mother had no love for herself because she became an alcoholic. As children they went to school with no love. Her little brother was the biggest casualty of all that. He was our Don Carlos, she said. My little brother, Jimmy.

She said love had to be passed on to you as a child. You see your reflection in a child's eyes. There is nothing in the world better than hearing a child laugh, nothing makes you happier than seeing food going into a child's mouth, she said. How could they send a boy out into the world with no love in him?

My brother, my reflection, she said.

You could hear the audience listening. You could

feel them getting angry on her behalf, crying with her. You could sense them leaning forward and agreeing with her, that a person has to have love inside them to receive it, otherwise love would have no reason to come looking for you. You could feel every mother in the place wondering if they had something to answer for, some moment where they had withheld love from a child. Everything they had done or not done, without knowing what they had done. Fathers too, like myself. That fear of looking back and wondering what could have been done differently, even when it's already too late.

She thanked the audience for listening to her life and bowed her head. And then, the big surprise came at the end, she sang a song. As she said herself afterwards, she murdered the song. It was all breathy and full of laughing, full of inhaling and coughing and lifting her voice up, as if she had to stand on a chair to get the notes down. It was a song about emigration. Everybody loved it. She forgot the words halfway through. All you could hear was her breathing up and down, like she was keeping the beat going. Then she remembered the words again and carried on all the way to the end, until her lungs were completely empty.

6

We're heading to the Botanic Garden and I get this mad phone call from Dublin. She has to listen to me saying hold it, Gerry, hold it. I'm with somebody. I'm in Berlin. She can hear me telling him that I'm not in the least bit interested in going to a school reunion, it's probably the last thing in the world I want to do. You can forget it. But they're all depending on me to be there, so he's saying, as if they can't have a school reunion without me. I tell him he can count me absent, but then he continues trying to persuade me by reminding me of some of the funny things that happened at school. Do I remember the two Kenny brothers and one of them had a big birthmark on his forehead, they used to call him Star Trek. Yeah. Hilarious. This is exactly the kind of stuff I don't want to hear about. I don't want to hear about the Lynch brothers either and how one of them is bald now working in the Pidgeon House power plant, or was he always bald, he asks, which is a ridiculous question, how could he be bald at school? I don't want to hear another word, so I end the call as quickly as possible and she wants to know what's going on.

You need friends, she says, why not meet your old pals from school?

Why not? I'll tell you why not.

Don't be like me, she says.

She knows I don't like looking back. She knows I'm always trying to put things behind me. She knows I'm trying to forget as much as possible, particularly things you can do nothing about. She says I'm still allowing my father to make my decisions for me. She says all my relationships with other men are copies of my relationship with my father. My father will be around for all eternity if I go on like this, she says, the world is full of men who are my father in disguise.

Be yourself, Liam, she says.

I'm not sure what Manfred thinks of all this talk going on inside his car and if he's the kind of person who keeps driving and not listening to what his passengers are saying to each other, or whether he hears it all and is only pretending to be the driver.

I tell her that I have no intention of going to a school reunion. Myself and my brother both wore the same coloured jumpers, given to us by my father, identical. They couldn't tell us apart. They thought I was my brother. They beat him up thinking it was me. I used to hate my brother not standing up for himself. I hated him because I loved him. I loved him and I hated him and now I love him even more because I had to pretend he was not my brother.

There is absolutely no way that I'm going to spend

thirty euros on a dinner in the Camden Hotel, sitting down with those savages, pretending it's all in the past. Even if it is in the past. The reunion of savages. Everybody laughing like savages and talking about how far they've come up in the world and how we're not savages any more.

Calm down, Liam. You're in Berlin.

I am calm.

She wants to know what my brother is doing now and so I fill her in on my family. Peadar, my older brother, is married and living at home and he's got a problem with water hammer. She has no idea what water hammer is, so I explain it to her. It's something my brother has inherited along with the house, it has to do with the old pipes, the old plumbing. Water starts hammering like a hammer due to air locking, if you run water or flush the toilet in two different places in the middle of the night, for example. It can wake up the whole house. It used to drive my father mad. It's virtually unheard of nowadays, a thing of the past which happens mostly in old houses.

I tell her that my brother has hardly done a thing to the house in the meantime, he's kept everything the way it was, unchanged. He wants to preserve it all according to his memory. He still has the same problem with mice that my father used to have. My brother's father is the same as my father, no difference, only that everybody has their own father to deal with. I still believe my father is after me. Even in the hotel sometimes, when I hear a door opening at night, I think he's coming to get me even though he's been dead for years and it can't be him, I checked. It was somebody who got the wrong door. Swedish tourists, I think, who thought I was in their room by mistake. And every time this happens to me, I discover nothing new, only that my father has better things to be doing than following me around for the rest of my life. I've been imagining him, that's all. It's only now that I know what I'm dealing with.

Liam, stop it, she says.

Also. The yellow door. The door I've been afraid of since childhood is not the door of the place where my father brought me when my mother was in hospital and I thought she was never coming back, the yellow door that still gives me the taste of custard at the back of my throat every time I pass by, and it's not the blue door of the school either, because the colour is irrelevant, so I'm told, it's not any of those doors but the door of my own home when I was a child that I should be coming to terms with and walking into without fear, whatever colour it was, dark green. A kind of deep green gloss that people had on doors in the past but which is not in use very much any more now.

7

There was a moment of sadness in the car from time to time that kept us from saying anything. We stopped talking quite suddenly and were silent, back to our own thoughts, looking out the window, arriving outside the gates of the Botanic Garden. As if there were no words left in the world, only the sound of the electronic door sliding back and the sound of traffic and the sound of Manfred getting out the wheelchair. All I could think about was how short the time was and how she would be dead so soon after that. You do your best not to think like this, but you can't help it. It's at the forefront of your mind, even when you think you've forgotten it and it seems like nothing is going to change, we're all going to live forever. There were occasions during the trip when she was close to crying and I wanted to cry with her, but I couldn't let myself. I wish I could. And I'm not sure sadness is the right word for what I felt as Manfred was helping her out of the car, getting her into the wheelchair and she was saying, thanks Manfred, you're a pet. It was bigger than sadness, I think. Something else, maybe the feeling that things were not quite as sad as they were meant to be, as though I was yet to discover what sadness was about and we had only briefly stepped outside normal time, waiting for real time to catch up again.

To be honest, I had no idea how to be sad. I couldn't find the words to describe what I was thinking in that kind of situation. What do you say when somebody is dying? What are you meant to talk about? You talk about nothing to do with dying, isn't that so? You say anything that comes into your head and pretend it's the furthest thing from your thoughts.

She was not afraid of talking about death and what it does to you. She said it took all the goodness out of life, hearing that it was over. Everything went black, she said. What was the point of it all? What was the point in all that knowledge inside her head coming to nothing? All the people. All the stories she collected. All the books she read. And what about all the good times? Did they all come to nothing as well? Or did they remain good times?

She said it was like a door closing.

She said it was like losing all the lovers she ever had, like losing her friends, losing her brother, like all the doors closing at once, like everybody leaving without a word, only this time it was herself that was leaving, she said.

That's what you do, Liam, you start saying good-bye. You go back over your life and you say goodbye to everyone, each one individually. You say good-bye to all the people you remember. All the things you had once in your possession, the jar of hand cream, your lipstick, your own thumbprint left in a tube of toothpaste. All the things you had that were never yours for keeps, only borrowed. The yellow curtains, Liam. The books. The shoes. The trace of yourself left behind. All the places you ever set foot in. All the houses you ever lived in, all those quiet rooms, all the fires at night, all the warm beds and the towels on the radiator.

And maybe there in Berlin with her was the first time I became aware of anyone close to me dying. I didn't say this to her, but when my own father died, I was too much in shock, I had spent so much time trying to get away from him that I was not mentally prepared for it when he disappeared. It felt as if he was only gone out to the garden to light a bonfire and he would be back any minute with the smell of smoke on his clothes asking me what I'd been up to. I felt suddenly very old when my father died. As if my life was gone past. His death was my death, so I thought, even though I obviously had to go on living, I had no option. I was still alive after him, but he might as well have taken me with him, I refused to believe it was him in the coffin. At his funeral I felt he was still fully present. My mother and all our relatives and everyone else in the church were in a different world and my father's brother, the Jesuit, was up on the altar saying his own brother was gone, the Lord had taken him to rest. I didn't believe any of those words. I wanted to run away from the church and all the people because they were suffocating me.

I think you need lessons in sadness. I had no idea what grief was at the time. I could see it in other people, but I didn't realise that I carried it with me all along. It was accumulating without me knowing it, like some dormant virus that can eventually erupt when you're least expecting it. When I saw my mother crying I could see everything, her whole life, her childhood, her memories, how much she must have been in love and how much she must have been loved, no matter how hard my father was on the family. Whenever people were sad, they showed all their happiness as well. I didn't think sadness should be revealed in a person, it was a weakness. I was only doing what everybody else was doing at the time, I thought, trying to avoid sadness. I was under the impression that everyone in Ireland was doing their best to pretend there was no such thing as sadness, singing, drinking, talking, telling stories, anything at all to keep themselves from looking sad, only when they were singing sad songs. I kept laughing at myself, laughing at the world, laughing at death, laughing at pain, laughing at things I liked, laughing at love and all those things that could hurt you if they were taken away, laughing at everything that makes you fall victim to sadness. I wanted to let everyone know that I was not afraid of my father dying, I was not bothered by any of that, so I told myself.

When my mother died I was still afraid to be sad. She was alone after my father died because her best friend, my father's brother, refused to visit her. All I knew how to do was to be her son. But he was her real companion, my father's brother, the Jesuit in the family. And then he stopped coming to see her. I didn't know the reason for this at the time. I knew there was a reason, but it's not something I worked out until much later. She would sit looking out at the back garden and wait for my father's brother, saying why does he not come and visit me? He was there at her funeral, the Jesuit. My father's brother. He came to say Mass for her. Although I was hardly present myself. I was there with the family, but I was more or less absent from then on, avoiding everything, shaking hands with my father's brother outside the church and not saying anything, wishing I was invisible, as if you cannot see your own life clearly when you're actually in it.

This time I was present.

Travelling around Berlin in the car for two days, pushing the wheelchair in through the gates of the Botanic Garden, for example, allowed me time to say goodbye to my own mother and father, in retrospect, from a distance. This time I was fully aware of what it means to lose somebody. And you know what, this may sound like the wrong thing to say, but there was something about Úna dying that triggered off something alive in me. It made me feel as though I was actually taking part in my own life for the first time. In fact, I think I was a bit elated being there near the end, with her. Even joyful. Exhilarated, you could say. Am I getting this right? It made me feel more myself. Or more like an exemption from myself, somebody released on parole or something like that, as if I never had to pay the fare again, as if all my debts were paid, that sort of feeling I had. I think. It felt as if none of the ordinary things mattered any more. That's what I thought. Or maybe it was the other way around, it was only the ordinary things that mattered, like buying the entrance tickets to the Botanic Garden and letting Manfred know that he had plenty of time to go for coffee, I would call him in a while when we were ready to leave again.

8

She told me about her love life. She said she first
had sex with a man when she was fifteen. He was
twice her age. She said she loved all the attention
her body got in her school uniform. How was she
supposed to know that he was a married man? She
said she was lucky that her father found out and
called her a slut and took her out of school and sold
his car and borrowed another car to take her to a
boarding school in the north of the country where
she would be out of danger and it was too cold and
damp to think about men. She said you could see
your breath when you went to sleep. And there was
nothing to think about only the Virgin Mary and
other girls.

This is not word for word. This is more like a
reconstruction, the back pages, she called it, made
up of some of the things she said about love and
sex and happiness, not all of it in Berlin. She loved
sex. Especially on Dublin afternoons, she said, with
the sound of buses going by and squeaking brakes.
She loved the sound of people's feet walking past

the basement window while the word fuck was flying out of her mouth.

Fuck was not a word she used that often.

She said love and sex were a bit like writing a novel, it had everything to do with fabrication. That's what I think she said. She said the best lover was the best storyteller, something like that. The problem with a lot of books, she said, was the writer trying to tell you what to feel. Writers getting the better of their readers, forcing themselves on their characters. Like one man she was with who told her that she was mistaken and that what happened between them was consensual, only that she was too young at the time to know the difference. She didn't like being told what to feel.

She had a boyfriend in London once who said she could not make love but she had to sit up in bed with a book afterwards. He hated me reading, she said, the way other people sat up in bed and smoked a cigarette. Which she did also, but with a book. He thought it was the biggest insult to a man. The book. He said she made sex look like doing the dishes and she couldn't wait to get back to her book, so he took out all the light bulbs. Every one of them, she said, just to make sure she stayed in the room and didn't escape with the book. But even in the dark I withdrew into my imagination, she said, like my mother did with my father. Even with no light in the room and no book to read I still crept away into a childhood corner of myself alone, rocking myself to sleep.

She said it was a great adventure, her love life. Sometimes she came across moments that were unforgettable, like seeing something from a moving train that you wanted to bring with you only it was already gone by and all you could do was try and write it down. She said it was delicious. Sex was delicious. I know it's an old word now, but it's an honest word, she told me, and I have no reason to doubt her. The meaning of delicious may not have changed all that much and sex may not have changed all that much either, it was all discovered in her time.

Delicious, she said.

She lived with a man for a long while who was a great reader and they went to lots of places together in Europe. He used to read aloud to her after breakfast, books that she had never heard of before. Things in books that she would never have noticed without talking about them and pointing them out to each other, like they were still learning to read. She said it was the only secure relationship she ever had and they could have got married but that would have put an end to all the travelling, wouldn't it? She said she didn't know what made her so afraid of getting married, only the fear of becoming her own mother. The wedding was called off and people were left holding their wedding gifts.

Because she always had the need to be alone again. She had to be herself. It was her greatest fear, not being herself, being restrained by the people she loved. Afraid of being in love because you might not be free. She could remember standing in the street listening to him telling her not to walk away, please, and all she could think of was keeping one foot on the pavement and the other foot off the pavement, everything swirling in her head, waiting for him to stop talking so she could walk away. Swirling was another word she used a lot and maybe that doesn't change much, it's still in the same place as before, like the word please, and the word finished and the word over. She used to sit alone in her room drinking wine like her mother. She would let the phone ring and not answer it, as if there was nobody in her life only the characters in the books she was reading. She thought there was something noble about being alone. She thought your family was where you trained how to be alone. She thought every person you loved would leave and you had to leave every person you loved. She had to be herself and being alone was the purest form of being yourself.

She said New York was a great place to be alone. She got to know a lot of people there and a lot of people knew her. In fact, people more often knew her when she didn't know them, people nodding to her as if she should remember them from somewhere. And then she would realise how much she needed people more than ever. Being alone was like denying the weather, something you could not avoid being in and out of, like having a mother and father, like having brothers and sisters, like religion, like being brought up in a Catholic school and needing to get away, being a writer.

She said she spent her life searching for men who were like her father. And one time late in her life she met an Irish truck driver who was like a real father. The trucker knew how to make up a story. The trucker with the false teeth, she said.

Love with false teeth.

Love without teeth, she said, so he could suck on my breasts.

I told her it was wrong to put all that into her book about the trucker. I wouldn't like those kind of details made public, if I had false teeth.

Jesus, I hope his wife didn't read it, she said.

His wife probably recognized the false teeth, I said.

Don't laugh about it, she said. That trucker was full of love and travelling. One night he came to me and he was unable to have sex, she said, he wasn't up to it. Too much on the road. So we just left it and went to sleep. And during the night I woke up to find him stroking my back. We didn't speak. He was sitting up in bed, gently stroking my back and I imagined him travelling across Europe, she said, off to England, across to France and Germany and down through Austria, all that mileage and all those road signs in different languages, all the faces of people he must have seen and spoken to, picking up his consignment of Italian tiles and bringing them all the way back along the big European roads, back on the ferry to Dublin. He travelled in his sleep, in silence, stroking my back, she said. Then he had to go home to his wife. He left me asleep and awake. He made himself a cup of tea. He didn't give himself time to drink it. He left the cup on the table. He walked out the door and continued on travelling.

I couldn't keep him, she said. I kept his letters. Beautiful letters, I kept them all. I brought them with me wherever I went travelling, a bundle of them in my suitcase all over the world. I kept them and read them from time to time, but I couldn't keep him. I couldn't keep anyone. The only way I had of keeping anything in my life was in my book.

9

I told her a bit about my love life. I didn't tell her when I first had sex, she didn't ask me. We talked about who I fell in love with when I was around nineteen. Her name is Emily and she is the mother of my daughter, Maeve. We talked about love and travelling and she wanted to know all about my back pages. How I took Emily down to Milltown Malbay in County Clare, when we were escaping from her boyfriend. Emily was living in a basement apartment with him and she invited me down for breakfast, a boiled egg. Her boyfriend was out, and before he came back, Emily asked me to take her away somewhere. Anywhere away. So that's what I did, I took her to away to Milltown Malbay.

It's a funny thing, you go somewhere abroad and right away you start talking about home, making connections. It's mad, isn't it. You go to Berlin and you end up talking about Clare and Milltown Malbay. She's sitting in her wheelchair and we talk about how much we both love the west of Ireland, Clare in particular. She has a house there, a small two-roomed cottage where she used to go to work on her books and walk across the Burren with Buddy. When she came back after living in London, she went down to Clare for the first time and she said it was like finding a place on the far side of the world that she had never heard of before, undiscovered.

We talk about the music festival in Milltown Malbay every summer. She remembers the musicians and the listeners on the street because there was never enough room and the pubs were turned inside-out.

I remember a piper sitting on a chair, she told me, brought out on the pavement. Men with their shirt sleeves rolled up to work the fiddle and women with accordions strapped across their chests and the knees going up and down like engines in the machine room of a ship. People bringing out drink and ham sandwiches to keep them going. She said there was always a man or a woman in the audience who got so excited by the speed of the music they would yelp and shout fair play to you, right in the middle of the tune, just to make sure they could be heard listening. And the pub where everybody was suddenly trying to get back in, like it was the only place in the world to be at that moment and there was no way a pub that small could accommodate the amount of people already inside. Where the crowd squeezing in at the door was like the people in London, she said, trying to get on the Underground. Only they were straining to hear a singer who had started up a song unaccompanied, with his eyes closed, holding on to the bar counter to steady himself.

I asked her about that pub, what was the name of it? But she could not remember the name. Was it a pub where women had to go through the kitchen to get to the bathroom at the back of the house, I wanted to know. And was there was a big bath in there with all these cracks. A huge bath with a million tiny hairline cracks in the enamel. She said she remembered a lot of bathrooms in the living quarters at the back of pubs and they all had cracked sinks and cracked tiles and mirrors that were gone freckled with black spots and plaster flaking off the ceiling and the geyser above the bath where the water came out boiling.

You must have seen the bath, I said to her. The bath with a million hairline cracks in the enamel.

Not that I remember, she said.

It was in that same pub, I said. I'm certain of it.

I was asking her all that because I was there myself at that festival, the year I escaped with Emily, possibly at the same time, listening to a man of that description standing at the bar, steadying himself on the counter. He was belting out this song with his eyes closed. And then who walks into the crowded bar, only Emily's boyfriend. I don't know how he could have known we were there, but Emily said she saw him squeezing his way through the crowd. I didn't actually see him myself, only that Emily looked up suddenly and said, shit. Then she took my hand and dragged me through the crowded bar, out the back, through the kitchen with the smell

54

of rashers and eggs and tealeaves. As we passed through I saw a range and an armchair in the corner with a holy picture on the wall above. Through the house Emily pulled me, into the bathroom where they had the cracked bath. She locked the door and that's where we stayed and waited. We could hear the man singing in the bar still, it must have been a hundred verses. You could hear a pin drop, as they say, as if there was nobody out there but the singer by himself alone, just the occasional cough or the sound of empty glasses, you know the way a barman puts a finger in each glass and sweeps them up with a clink, three or four glasses in one go, as many fingers as he has available. Emily was sitting on the side of the bath with the million hairline cracks, wearing a green dress and black boots and a light-brown cardigan with the top buttons open. Her hair was long and she had lots of freckles. She was playing with the chain, swinging the grey stopper around while I was standing with my back to the door. We didn't say a word. I was not smiling or laughing or anything like that, and nor was Emily, only that she lifted her shoulders as if to say, what else can you do?

I don't remember how we got out of there in the end. All I remember is Emily sitting on the edge of the bath with all the hairline cracks and whispering to me that maybe there was time to have a quick bath together while we were waiting, only that there was no soap except ivy soap and that was for washing the floor, not for washing your body. What a pity we didn't bring a candle. And what a pity we didn't bring our drinks with us at least, Emily added.

There was a picture of Pope John the Twenty-third and John F. Kennedy in the bathroom with us. Maybe the only one left in Ireland. The picture was quite faded with the steam from so many baths. John F. Kennedy had his head tilted to one side and there was a water cloud covering half his face. Pope John held his hand up in a blessing and his white robe was gone brown, buckled up with age. I know that because Emily asked me to look at the picture carefully while she was having a piss.

Listen to the song outside, she said.

And then I ended up bringing Emily for a bath after all, the next day. The seaweed baths. Out along the coast, a place with blue painted doors and blue window frames, where people came from all over the world, men and women from Germany and Scandinavia, in their dressing gowns. The centre for hot seaweed baths. They gave Emily a cubicle to herself with a bath she could not even put her toes into first it was so hot, full of brown seaweed, like brown leather straps. There was steam everywhere and echoes of people splashing water around their bodies in other cubicles, talking to each other in Swedish over the wooden partitions. When Emily eventually lay back in the bath, she said it felt quite slimy at first, a bit like floating in cod liver oil, but she liked it because it's meant to be good for your health, you'll never get rheumatism, all those promises going back hundreds of years. Her face was flushed from the heat and she played with the seaweed straps all around her body, making a long brown, underwater dress for herself with seaweed straps around her thighs and seaweed straps covering her breasts and going around her shoulders. You'd never forget the smell of seaweed either, it stays in your memory, you recognize it instantly as soon as you get to the coast. Emily's skin was very smooth afterwards, I remember, I don't really have the word for it exactly, so smooth it was almost not there, more like holding your hand under running water. And afterwards, to rinse the oily feeling from her body we went out to the Pollock Holes near Kilkee, Pollies they're called, these natural pools in the rocks where people in dressing gowns go swimming when the tide is out, because the water left behind in those pools is so clear and warm and deep and calm and full of minerals. And all the time I was looking around me, searching up and down the shore to see if we were being followed.

10

We had the Botanic Garden to ourselves, give or take. We were like any other tourists, really, looking around, taking pictures. Apart from her being in a wheelchair, the people there would have thought nothing unusual, only that she was not up to walking, that's all. She kept the cap on, so nobody knew what was going on underneath. We were unseen mostly, apart from a few onlookers here and there, more interested in all that stuff coming to life around us. It was warm, you could feel the sun pulling things out of the earth. The air was full of cross-fertilization.

We brought our own summer with us, she said.

It was spring, in fact, but she did that sometimes, quoting words from a song or a book. I didn't always know what she meant, because she was not speaking to me directly but remembering a random line that made sense on its own, without being part of a conversation.

Unless she was saying that you bring your own weather with you. Could that be right?

I got the tickets in the small cottage, a gate lodge. She said it reminded her of going to the zoo in Dublin, with the entrance through black turnstiles beside a thatched cottage in the Phoenix Park, only there was no smell of elephants in the air here. We were both given a brochure through the window, what we could expect to find coming back to life again. There was a trail mapped out with the most beautiful places not to be missed.

They were lovely gardens, I have to say. But the thing is, I might not have seen everything in Berlin with my own eyes, but through her eyes, for the last time. Our conversation was full of last things. I was here with her for the last time. And I would say that ninety percent of what you see is ultimately for other people.

She called the trees and the shrubs by name, as if she knew them personally. I remember them like you never forget a face, but I can't tell you what they are unless I read the names on the plaque or someone tells me. The copper beech, she said. As if it was the only copper beech tree ever, the same one she had seen many times elsewhere in Ireland or Europe or North America, and it had come to say goodbye to her at the Botanic Garden.

There was a wide path that led between a mansion on one side and a lake with water lilies and ducks on the other. It was how you would imagine botanic gardens, maybe that's why I didn't notice much, only the conservatories in the distance and a water tower behind it. It made me think of those enormous jigsaw puzzles we used to get of beautiful gardens.

People don't have much time for them any more because they take over too much space and one or two of the thousand pieces always went missing before you got finished, if ever. And my father always thought it was a terrible waste of time. You had to make the most of your life, puzzles and board games were nothing but time-wasting.

The conservatories were tropical. It was a different country in there. They keep the place at thirty-five degrees all year round. And the humidity, we were walking into a heat wave. They had radiators lined up underneath the glass, and there was steam blowing down from the pipes to give you an impression of where all these plants came from. She said it was like a huge glass cathedral. You could hear running water, like prayers. Not that I've been there, she said, but the rainforest reminds me of the interiors of a church. In fact, all those silent plants together under one glass roof made me think of what it must have been like before we were here, on earth, ages back. Some of the flowers you might have seen before in a florist or a petrol station, though I never saw a coffee plant before. It was good to see them where they belonged, in a more natural habitat. More authentic, undisturbed.

And still there was something missing, I thought, the sounds of birds maybe, a few shrieks here and there, like monkeys up above, in the canopy. I was half expecting to see an iguana or a snake, a pair of eyes at least, staring out through the foliage occasionally. There were a few flightless birds brought in especially from the tropics to keep the insects down.

Beneficial species, they call them. Apart from them there were only a few sparrows that managed to get in through the windows, doing no harm. I think people were primarily there for the horticulture and the peace of mind. It's the absence of noise they were looking for. It occurred to me that this would be a great place to work, testing the soil and checking the temperature, picking off dead leaves, avoiding over-crowding, making sure the plants have everything they need and thinking of them as your own family. You could belong to a place like this, I thought. We saw one or two gardeners walking around in their inner world. There was a couple sitting on a bench meditating, either that or sleeping, it was hard to tell. And a man with a camera on a tripod taking close-up photographs of an orchid. He obviously had permission to do that. All in all it was perfect for a visit, only the environment was not right. It was not long before her breathing started giving trouble.

I can't breathe in here, she said. I'll suffocate.

She preferred being out in the open with the trees, everything afresh. She asked me to push the wheel-chair off the path, right into a meadow of cowslips. That's what I remember. She said cowslips as if they had disappeared last year in the west of Ireland and now they were coming up out of the ground in Berlin. They were part of her childhood and she must have been confused by her whereabouts. The ground was soft and the tyres sank into the earth and she sat there a while, sinking and thinking. What she said could easily have been said to the cowslips without me being there at all.

I have a photo of her there to back it up, reaching down to touch the cowslips. Also a short video clip of her taken on my phone, more or less stationary, huddled in her black coat and the see-through bag hanging on the handle of the wheelchair.

She was going to say something. About her childhood. She said you can't possibly stop yourself from looking back.

I agreed with her. You can't avoid coming across things in your life that are pointing backwards, objects that surface in front of you, while you're not looking, while you're trying to delete things that cannot be deleted. Photographs, for example. Little bits of evidence that turn up where they don't belong in your life any more.

What are you talking about?

Just when you're trying to move forward, that is.

Rubbish. I'm talking about the truth, she said. Not hiding anything. It takes too much energy to conceal things, Liam. She could no more stop telling her story than she could stop breathing. That's all I was ever doing, she said, breathing and telling. Unless you want me to be silent like a gardener and keep my mouth shut. As if gardeners don't breathe. And the idea of her becoming a gardener instead of a writer was never very realistic. She said she once heard about a writer in America who was told by a friend that looking back makes you go crazy. But the writer ignored all that advice and went straight home to look back and write a book about school, just to stop himself going crazy.

I can no more stay silent than a horse can run backwards, that's what she said.

She remembered a man trying to reverse a horse out of an alleyway when she was a girl. The sight of a horse and cart was gone from the streets now and she wondered what was the point in remembering things that were always going to disappear. It was one of the things she collected as a child. Because she was a writer even before she could read, long before she ran down and told the woman in the shop, I can read, I can read. And the woman in the shop said good girl, aren't you great now? They had to be careful what they said in future because she had turned herself into a collector. Collecting all kinds of useless things, hiding them like favourite stones under her pillow.

The man collecting the scrap metal had the horse and cart in the alleyway. I was nothing but a girl, she said, standing in the street with one foot on top of the other. I had nothing better to do than watching the man trying to back the horse and the heavy load of metal out. I copied everything down in my head, she said, the wheels, the leather belt tied around the axle for no reason, the hind legs with white ankle socks and the eyelashes like a beauty queen. The man was standing in front of the horse negotiating, she said, but the horse had no wish to go backwards. The horse was afraid time was going to start going backwards from there on and his legs were only designed to go forward, I knew that, she said. The horse kept rearing its head up, trying to look back over its shoulder at something it didn't want to do. She remembered the fear in the horse's eyes. The slippery sound of hooves on the cobbles. That was the first thing I ever collected, she said, the day of the horse refusing to go backwards. It took the man ten minutes, maybe an hour, maybe all day in her memory. Again and again he tried to coax the horse. A white string of spit was suspended from its mouth, she said. In the end the metal collector had to put a sack over the horse's head and move forward and backwards until the horse was confused enough about the direction of time that he finally agreed to come out, a bit like a man coming down a ladder. And that's how I started asking questions, she said, because everything had to be turned backwards, until it was out in the open. Until the horse was a horse again, trotting off along the street and the cart was tilted to one side under the weight of metal.

11

We're in the field of cowslips and she asks me to
take off her shoes. She wants to tell me something
that she's never figured out before. Something that
happened between her mother and father.

Liam, she says. I want to stand up.

Here?

Can you take off my shoes?

You can't do that, Úna. It's too cold.

I need to feel the grass, she says.

What about pneumonia? What if she gets ill and
people ask me why I took her shoes off in the park,
in May?

Your childhood is in the grass, she says.

I know this is not good, but I'm already undoing
the white laces, taking off the shoes and socks and
helping her to stand up in her bare feet, because I
can't stop her going through her collection.

She remembers waking up one night with the
sound of knocking, she says. She got up and went
downstairs because her mother and father were not

in bed. She was only four or five at the most, and she understood nothing of what she was about to see in front of her.

There was a light on down there, coming in from the kitchen door left open. My mother and father were in the living room, she says. My mother was sitting on my father's knee, facing him, not sideways but straight ahead, with her legs out. I could see one of her bare knees. She was knocking his head against the wall and I thought she was killing him. I stood at the bottom of the stairs not knowing what to do, she says, because your mother can't be doing something like that without explanation. She had her hands in his hair and I saw her banging his head against the wall again and again. She was shouting at him at the same time, not words that I knew from before, nothing people would have said in the shop but some terrible language that you could only hate somebody with.

My mother saw me standing in the doorway, she says, watching her. And the look in her eyes was furious. I was afraid of her. I thought she was going to stop killing my father and kill me instead, she says, for being there, for seeing what was going on, for being a child watching.

I'm listening to her, holding the red canvas shoes in my hand.

My mother sighed, she says, and said my father had done a terrible thing. Your father has been very bold, my mother said, he has to be punished. She turned back to face him. Never let me see you do that again, my mother said to him, then she banged

66

his head against the wall again. Very, very bold. Never do that again, ever, ever, ever.

Her father didn't look at her, she says. His mouth was open, like he needed water. I clearly remember the moonlight coming in from the kitchen and the crucifix on the wall and my father letting a word out of his mouth that was not a word at all but the sound of great pain.

I'm only telling you what I saw, Liam.

She was told to go back up to bed. None of the other children were awake, she says, she was the only one who saw this happening. I was afraid to tell them, she says. I lay in bed trying to work out what my father had done that my mother would hit his head against the wall, and him not arguing back.

Úna. Please let me put your shoes back on.

Why didn't they tell me they were in love?

Your feet must be freezing.

What was so wrong with saying the word love? It took me years to realise that they loved each other, once. It was something I worked out backwards, like coming down the ladder. And it wasn't moonlight either, only the fluorescent light left on in the kitchen.

Why didn't they just say?

She's looking down at the cowslips.

Why did they make up that stupid story of punishment? Why didn't my mother say they were only pretending? Why didn't she stroke the side of my father's face and say they were only playing and that she was going to make him some cocoa and we would all go back to sleep? It would not have been such a lie. And maybe it might have prevented what

67

was coming. Because when you're a child, she says, you believe everything, you take people at their word. You feel responsible for your father and mother, she says. Everything that happens to them is happening to you. When they're afraid you're afraid. When they're happy you're happy. And when they can't talk about things, you will not be able to talk about them either.

Finally she lets me put her shoes on again.

Her mother's eyes would not let her in after that, she says. It hurt my mother to look at the world without my father being at home. My mother was blinded, she says, because he was coming home without being there any more. Her eyes were closed even when they were open, she could not see a thing in front of her. My mother could do nothing but read books, she says. I remember her, she says, sitting on the rug spread out in the Phoenix Park, looking for my father in the book she was reading. There was a sign with a finger pointing to the Zoo. The monkeys were calling. Your father is not coming. And your mother is never going to find him in Tolstoy. There was nothing for me to do, she says, but to keep watching the world going by at random. I saw a woman and a man lying on the grass kissing. I saw the steam coming up from the brewery. I saw crows fighting over the crust of a sandwich gone pink with jam. I saw a man tucking his trouser leg into his sock and getting on his bike, whistling, 'From a Jack to a King'. I recognized the song and it made the day very sad, because my mother was going in the opposite direction to the song, waiting for my father until she fell asleep with the roof of the book over her face. My brother said she was dead and I said she was drunk, so we ran away and left her there alone. We took off our shoes and ran across the grass quietly. I remember everything, she says, because I stood on a beer cap and it was like a shell under my foot, the sharp edges left a star-shaped mark.

12

There is a bit of confusion over gates. I have this conversation with Manfred on the phone which is basically me telling him that he's not at the gate and him telling me that he is at the gate. What gate? Obviously, we're at the wrong gate. He tells us not to move, he will drive around to our gate and I tell him to stay where he is, there is no point in switching gates. So we revert to the original plan. We'll come to his gate, where we were supposed to be in the first place. I tell him it might take another while and he tells me there's no rush, he will be waiting for us, at the main gate.

She keeps stopping every few metres and I get the impression that she doesn't want to leave. She wants to stay in these gardens and not move on in time. It's warm. The sun is out and there is great shelter here, no wind. We come across all kinds of shrubs and trees that she recognizes and others that she doesn't recognize. She tries to make out the information on the plaque underneath to see where they originated and whether she has been there yet.

Now and again she reaches out her hand to feel some of the new leaves. She rubs the leaves between her thumb and forefinger and smells the scent. Then she puts her hand up for me to get the scent as well.

And while we're stopping to compare each shrub, we get talking about what it's like to be a child and what it's like to be a parent.

My parents were careless, Liam. They didn't care.

She's pulling at the branches of one of the shrubs and then lets go, so the shrub springs upright, shaking itself like an animal.

I think she's being too hard on her parents. When you're a father yourself, you don't have all that much say, I tell her. You can't be made responsible for everything down the line that's out of your hands. All you can do is obey the rules of what a child needs. You love your child regardless, but you still have to live yourself. I'm speaking for the parent here. Because that's something I know a bit about, being a father.

I'm at the mercy of the future, that's what I'm trying to explain to her. She's at the mercy of the past and I'm at the mercy of the future.

She raises her hand to let me know that I'm pushing the wheelchair too fast, there's something she missed. I have to reverse a bit. The bushes look exactly alike to me but she can tell the difference.

Getting born is something that's done to you, she says.

We're retracing our steps at this point, back past the field of cowslips. We can see the tiered gardens and the symmetrical hedges and the lawns between

71

the paths. We come back past the statues of the naked boy and the naked girl on each side. And the conservatories, the green water-tower on top of the red-bricked base in the background, it's in one of the photographs.

That was one of the reasons why she decided to have no children herself, so I gather. She didn't want to be her own mother. No more than I wanted to be my own father, so to speak, even though you can't help it.

She didn't want to feel responsible for the future. The population, she calls it.

I think she wanted to stop the future at herself. She wanted to be her own child, her own offspring. She wanted women to have the freedom to be themselves and not have to bear children if they didn't want to, to become artists and writers and musicians instead of surrendering their entire lives and rearing children like her mother did. She didn't believe all that stuff they told Emily about not having anything during the birth, no epidurals, embracing the pain, as they call it, because it makes you bond better with your child. Úna wanted to bond with the world, I suppose. She wanted the right to do things to herself. She didn't want to do the same to a child that was done to her, in other words. She didn't want her own reflection following her around for the rest of her life. She wanted only to be responsible for herself, in her own lifetime, her own person, her own body.

I'm gathering all this now, in retrospect.

She had enough trouble breaking out of her family plot without starting a new one. Your family, your country, where you were brought in. The entry point, she calls it. It stays with you, it's after you no matter where you go.

It's in your shoes.

She wanted the freedom to write and tell the story. She says your life is your story. And she's often said this before, in public, in Ennis and Aspen. Sure what are we only stories. That's all we are, Liam, only walking stories. We are at the mercy of our stories and our children and our families. Because that's all there is, the stories we tell about ourselves, the stories that are told about us, the stories we tell about each other. And the stories withheld. The stories we have to make up because they have been kept from us.

13

There was a great freedom in being so open with her. I told her things that I would never have said to anyone else alive, all kinds of things that she was not going to remember. In those last few days, I could tell her everything because she was going to take it all away with her, off my shoulders.

Is there something you're not telling me?

She stops the wheelchair with one foot skidding on the ground. She tells me to stand in front of her. Liam, where I can see you. Look into my eyes. Is there something you want to tell me?

Because she has the ability to reach all the way inside my head and find out what she wants. With or without my consent. It's one of those things she picked up from her father. In through the eyes, take what you like. He was a famous journalist and she became a famous writer after him. Her father had those eyes that everybody wanted to be seen by. He made people forget about themselves and hand over things they never even knew they had. She inherited that gift of being able to walk through an open door and help herself. Go through people's belongings without them even knowing. Anything that remained concealed, closed to the public, even those things you were keeping from yourself, she had a good guess at. Her eyes won't let go. That's what made her a writer, you came out of a conversation with her feeling a bit ransacked. She was interested in everything that was undiscovered. Undisclosed. And there was no stopping her from working out what she didn't know, by intuition, by multiple choice. By remaining silent and letting you walk your way into the empty space.

You can tell me, Liam.

She knows my eyes have no locks on them and people can wander in and out like they're at an auction. She knows I want to talk about my life but it feels a bit like stealing from myself.

That's impossible, she says.

I feel my life is stolen goods when I talk about it.

You can't steal your own property, Liam.

I don't know what is my own property, I tell her. I always thought my life was my own property and my daughter was in it, but now I'm not so sure any more that you can be the owner of your own life.

It's bad for you to keep things to yourself, she says. It will burn a cigarette hole in your head.

All I have to talk about is my daughter.

Go on, she says.

My daughter is having doubts, I tell her. Maeve. She's twenty-five and very successful at her work, she loves what she's doing, but there's something wrong. She's with one of those online companies and they keep telling her that she's part of the family, the company is her family now. I know it's only what they say to make employees feel at home in the workplace, your new family. But she's got all this doubt. I think she's picked it up from me. Something missing.

Like what?

Her real family.

The main gate is in sight now, with the traffic beyond. We're stopped right in the middle of the wide path, with the lake on one side and the mansion on the other side, switched around this time, from left to right. And I'm telling her all this stuff about my daughter, asking if there are human reasons for everything.

You're blowing this out of proportion, Úna says.

I tell her my daughter has been asking questions.

What questions?

Maeve wants to know who she is. She's asking all about me and Emily, her mother. The back story, she doesn't believe us.

She's nervous about the wedding, Liam, that's all.

She's thinking of calling it off, I tell her.

You can't let her do that, Úna says.

She's having second thoughts.

You can't let her have second thoughts, Liam. You can't let her cancel the wedding, that's what happened to me. It was a perfectly good wedding and a perfectly good marriage only that I called it off. I thought it was too good to be true. Liam. Listen to me. You tell Maeve from me, not to call off that wedding. Please. She'll spend the rest of her life having second thoughts.

Maybe she's not ready for it.

You're far too protective, Liam. Your precious little daughter. You're all over her.

I don't want to let her down.

You're at the mercy of your own child, Liam. Come on, get a grip of yourself. That whole fatherhood instinct. Fathers loving their daughters to bits. It's so repulsive, I'm going to get sick. Think of how other people feel, she says, that cosy little relationship you have going together, excluding everyone else. You're refusing to let her grow up. That's what you're doing, Liam. You want her to remain a child. The child you want her to be. I bet you can't even let her cross the street without holding her hand.

I love her.

What? You love her like an overheated room, she says. You love her like that glass cathedral over there, thirty-five degrees. You're suffocating her.

You hate me talking about Maeve, don't you?

She's getting married, Liam. She's out of your hands, let her go.

You can't stand my daughter getting all the attention, is that it?

Liam. I'm only helping you to own your life.

Manfred is waiting for us. I can see him standing on the far side of the gate, staring into the park, keeping an eye out for a wheelchair. I begin to push the wheelchair towards the gate but she stops me once more.

Hold it, she says. Come here. Let me give you a hug.

So then I have to lean down and try to work out how to embrace her in the wheelchair. She lets go of the see-through bag with all her belongings and throws her arms out. And as I'm going into her arms, it's hard for me to know where to put my own arms because they won't go around her, the wheel-chair begins to back away from me and I have to hold on to her bag, sliding down between us. I have to catch the bag with my knees. It seems too premed-itated to put on the brakes or to put the bag down for a moment and do this properly. So I just impro-vise. I try my best to hold on to everything without making it look like I care too much about things that don't matter right now. She reaches forward to pull my face down onto her shoulder for everybody in the Botanic Garden to see. I lean in towards her as much as I can but it's only the side of her face that I'm in contact with and her arms are pulling me down further by the neck than it's possible for me to go without the wheelchair rolling away. Her breathing is loud, I can hear the rhythm of it.

I'm still here, Liam, she says.

All I can say is nothing. I mean that, not a word. I'm leaning right across her in silence, trying not to hurt her, in spite of the fact that she's in such pain and not saying a thing about it, only withholding it. As well as not having a son of her own to embrace, or even her brother.

Manfred is standing at the gate with his hands behind his back. His feet are placed apart. His chest

78

is out. It looks like he's been standing in that position for some time now, watching us. He doesn't move. I wave to let him know that we're on the way, we're coming, but he remains still, as if he has not seen us yet. He continues looking straight at us, as though he's going to carry on waiting for us to appear.

14

The will she made. She made a will that was like a short story with all the characters of her life. It was her way of gathering around the people she was close to and speaking to them personally after she was gone, leaving them a couple of words along with whatever she was intending to give them. From the way she wrote the will, it sounded like she was still very much present, keeping up the conversation. As if she was still telling people what to do with their lives. As if she still wanted to know what was going on and how everybody was doing. What was the news. Who was going to be the next president of America, that kind of thing.

She wanted to die with no money on her hands. She left most of her money to charity with children in mind.

Her last will and testament. You could say it allowed her to carry on living in some way, for a few more pages at least. People don't disappear and stop talking suddenly when they die, do they? You carry on having the same conversation you were having before, in fact, the relationship you have with someone keeps growing, she said, only that you understand them much better after they're gone. They become even more of a story that you want to keep telling.

She has forgotten nobody. Everyone is remembered, personally. The words she chose for each individual were non-transferable.

What she said to me in her will was already said alive. Very simple. I'll never forget you bringing me to Berlin as long as I live. So thank you, Liam. Thank you. Thank you.

What can you say to that? No, it's me alive who has all the reasons to remember and say thank you. Of course, it's not possible to answer back. Not verbally anyway. She's having the last word, and none of us have the right to reply, not until we write our own will.

A list of things, that's what she said all writing was. Making a list. Your own list. Her final list.

I give and bequeath, it said at the top of the page, with the beneficiaries listed underneath along with the sums of money or property. She wrote the will after she returned to Dublin from Berlin and it was clear from the document that she had given it a lot of thought. She spent time carefully thinking up what she would say to us.

In loving memory of many pints.

For a new teapot after the one I broke.

For all the messages left on my phone which were like a fire to come home to and I'm sorry if I didn't reply at the time.

81

For a new pair of gloves. Although. That seemed to be more like a private joke and the person receiving the money for gloves must have had some story which only they would remember.

For looking after Buddy with such great fondness and being so good to him when I was away.

For wit and imagination.

For putting up with my sourness. For not getting angry whenever I just turned my back and picked up the newspaper and ignored everyone else at the dinner table as if I was better off alone.

For the time we got soaked, remember. When we were watching the waves. The anger in them.

For the time I got lost in Wicklow and I couldn't find the cottage and then I did find it after all.

For knowing everything about Dublin that I could not remember. All the things I would never think of without the company of somebody else to talk to. For reminding me where exactly the door to the ladies used to be in Kehoe's, before it was all changed. For remembering the crankiest barman in the world. For remembering what was there once in Dublin, all the streets and the corners and the women selling flowers and Bewley's, when it was still Bewley's and you could spend all day reading and drinking the same cup of coffee and eating the same cherry bun gone pink, only looking up every now and again to see who was who. What order the shops were in, with the bookshop still on Grafton Street and the only restaurant we could afford on South Anne Street. And the time we went for a big slap-up dinner in a fancy place intending to do a

82

runner without paying, but the meal was far too heavy in my stomach even to walk, so we got up from the table in a great hurry and ran to the door, only for me to change my mind at the last minute, so I ran to the bathroom instead, like I needed to go very badly, and came back and paid the bill after all. For those things I would have forgotten by now. For remembering Dublin when the city was nothing but a few pubs. For remembering the people and the order they stood in at the bar and the type of things they were saying and God knows where they are now?

For keeping the time. For keeping the time we were in.

She looked after all the people who were important to her. She distributed some of her furniture and itemized certain things, remembering particular people who used to visit her and where they normally sat at the table, what cups they drank from. To one person she left her second-best chair, for example, which was obviously another private joke they were having a laugh over during her lifetime and long after.

To various people she left money for pure friendship, for their songs, for inspiration, for being so encouraging and supportive. For allowing me to be myself, she writes, for giving me the lift when I needed it. Her will was full of optimism. She left a lot of praise for people, reminding them that how good they were was far more important than how bad they were. She said they were to remember the good times, the future would take care of itself.

I've no idea if people followed her instructions. There was no way of compelling them to keep her furniture or to spend the money in any particular way, legally. And converting the money into cash usually gets rid of any personal significance. Or maybe they converted the money into memory, blowing it on something unspecified like going on the tear and getting rat-arsed and drugged-up on her behalf, if that's the case. Who knows what the money was spent on in the end? They could even pay the car tax or allow the money to flow into the general household budget and spend it on frozen pizzas in memory of her. Which was all fine, for all I know, as long as they actually felt the money in their pockets for a moment at least.

To a fellow writer she gave the yellow curtains she bought in New York, drifting in the open window.

To another writer friend she left a sum of money for all the walks not yet walked without a map.

For Noleen she left money to keep on travelling.

15

I was thinking about her shoes, the shoes she had on in Berlin. The red canvas shoes. I'll remember them as long as I live. I wonder where they went to. Because the shoes keep you. They keep you always. After you've stepped out of them. Is this making any sense? Your presence remains in the shoes after you take them off and you park them under the bed at night. You might as well still be in them, even when you're not. They look like they'll start walking by themselves.

Maybe the shoes were given away along with her clothes, everything dispersed, distributed, whatever word you can use for personal things that cannot be put in a will or passed on to anyone else. I wonder did her shoes end up in a charity shop somewhere, in with all the other people's stuff, in with the second-hand smell left behind in their clothes and their shoes? In with all those things that people wore and had regard for once. One of those places where people root around in other people's belongings, to see if there is anything of value. Where you find things like a doll's house, or a game of Monopoly still intact, things like wall lamps that are perfectly good only missing the second one to make up a matching pair. Things that creep up on you like St Patrick's Day medals that you would not have seen since you were in school, or a hurling stick with grass stains which somebody has signed, or those luminous statues of St Christopher that people used to stick onto the dashboard of their car. My own father had one because he was obsessed with safety. Teapots with animal faces, and Toby jugs, and a mug with Lady Di and Prince Charles when they were young and getting married with the handle missing. A milk bottle for the World Cup. People not paying much attention to anyone else, only occasionally looking about to see what other people had found. As if you don't know what you want until somebody else wants it. People going through a trolley full of old DVDs while somebody else is plugging in a perfectly good hairdryer to see if it's still working and not just blowing out cool air instead of hot.

And all the shoes, racks of shoes that people wore all over the country, who knows where they've all been. Shoes that carried people across the world, on trains, around airports and shopping centres and cinemas, shoes that tell the story of their journeys. Shoes that people gave away for no good reason and that had nothing wrong with them, completely new-looking, maybe only briefly lived in, maybe the wrong size, ill-fitting. Runners, loafers, deck shoes, boots with fur around the rim, shoes with heels you cannot imagine anyone wearing, lots of ordinary shoes and lives you cannot imagine anyone living.

I remember once she told me about driving down the country and going into a house where an artist had glued shoes up against the wall. She wrote about that in one of her books. How she came across this exhibit that an artist had made with shoes. I wish I had seen it myself. All along the wall, right up to the ceiling. And maybe that's what I'm thinking, that maybe her shoes ended up in some kind of montage, that they might have been kept by someone, those red canvas shoes.

They were frayed a bit and slightly faded, with the shape of her feet indented, the toes, the heel gone shiny and worn down from contact with the street. And yes, one broken white lace. That's how I remember them.

16

She was helping me to look back and deal with my memory. There was this thing I told her about which was going on in my family. I'm still not sure exactly what it was, because nobody talked about it very much. That's what happens to people who don't talk, she said, they behave the same as their own fathers and mothers and father's brothers, in my case. I tried my best not to be like my father and I ended up being more like my father's brother. The Jesuit. He never said very much. He spoke only when absolutely necessary.

Everybody loved the Jesuit in the family. I had an aunt on my father's side who left all she had to the Jesuits and the donkey sanctuary. Not that anyone should ever be expecting prize money from relatives when they die, or pegging their memory of a person to the sum received. Which is far from the truth in this case, because my aunt was very kind to us. We loved her. Me and my brother will never forget the time she took us down to Cork to see the donkey sanctuary for ourselves. I know it meant a lot to her. Also the Jesuits meant a lot to her.

It was not long after my aunt lost her husband, so she was still in mourning and didn't want to travel all that distance alone. She took us with her for the company. We will never forget that journey to Cork because my aunt was in tears sometimes while she was driving, telling us about everything, the Rock of Cashel coming into view around the bend. We never imagined that anything as old as the Rock of Cashel could still exist in our time. I think it made my aunt feel better to be travelling. And then the car stalled on the steepest hill in Ireland, in Cork City. I can still remember the sound of the engine straining and her laughing, a frightened laugh that frightened us, thinking she had forgotten the handbrake and we were going to roll all the way back to where we came from. Until she stopped at an angle in the middle of the street and we got out. She said she knew somebody in Cork who could point the car forward again, back down the hill. She brought us for fish and chips which was something we never had the taste of before because my father was against food that was not cooked at home. Fish and chips was something foreign to our family and we never even spoke about it or wanted it. Fish and chips was for other people, not us. So having fish and chips in Cork was something I could never forget. It was the greatest kindness. Like something left to me in a will, something I can keep, something I can't spend.

My aunt had the best smile that I ever saw, mostly

with her eyes. She was very generous. She put us up in a hotel in Cork. I think it was the first time we ever stayed in a hotel. She had her room and we had our room, though I had to sleep with my brother in the same bed and we tried our best to stay separate, as far away from each other as possible. We said good night to my aunt, but then we got up again. We got dressed and went downstairs, I don't really know why. I think we just wanted to be awake. We thought it was a waste to sleep in Cork. We didn't talk, but I knew what my brother was thinking and he knew what I was thinking. We agreed without agreeing, saying only the least words necessary. We left the room and went down the stairs to explore, I suppose, that's what we called it without saying the word.

We walked through the reception, out the door. I think we wanted to see the street in darkness, the front porch of the hotel with the lights on, one missing. We wanted to see people, anybody out there smoking, the smell of cigarettes in the open. The air in the street at night. Our own breath like smoke. And cars going by. Guessing by the headlights and the sound of the engine what model it could be, particularly motorbikes, what CC they were and what the maximum speed was on the speed dial.

And as we were standing there, we saw a man and a woman coming out of the hotel together holding hands. It took a few seconds to realise that we knew them. There was my aunt, walking towards us. I thought she must be coming to tell us to go to bed, we had no permission to be out there on the street. The man she was with was wearing a light-grey suit, so we didn't recognize him at first. It was my father's brother, the Jesuit. Even though he was not dressed as a Jesuit, we knew it was my father's brother because we recognized his face and his voice. He had only recently been at the funeral of my uncle, my aunt's husband, a few weeks before that, saying Mass for him.

I was sure they must have seen us standing next to the railings. We were so obvious. I could think of no excuse for being out in the street after we had already said good night. But then they passed us by. I suppose they were not expecting us to be there. Even though my father's brother looked straight at me, in the eyes, he didn't recognize me, he thought we were just boys at the railings.

My aunt was smiling. Her smile was full of sadness and happiness, if you can imagine that. When I saw my aunt at the funeral of her husband, my uncle, she could hardly walk, she had to be carried, people holding her arms on both sides. One of her shoes came off on the steps and they had to put it back on again for her, because she had no feeling in her feet, they were not even touching the ground any more. I could see what grief was and I was confused by it. I didn't understand how it could be so close to happiness as well.

Maybe grief and happiness were the same thing, I thought.

My father's brother, the Jesuit, put his elbow up in the air and she slipped her arm inside, hooking.

That's what we saw, my brother and me. We saw them walking away, arm in arm. We saw them stopping at the end of the street. My aunt leaned her head against his shoulder and they disappeared. I had no thoughts in my head only does he have sweets in his pocket. That's what my brother was thinking about as well, both of us thought everything together, identical. Did my father's brother have sweets in his left pocket when he was walking away with my aunt on his arm, wine gums usually? We didn't say anything to each other. We couldn't tell anyone, not my mother, not my father, not the Jesuit, not my aunt, not even ourselves. We were afraid to be found out. We didn't know what to do with the information, so we pretended that we saw nothing, only cars and people passing by. We went back upstairs and put our pyjamas on and tried to sleep, side by side, he was always taking the blankets.

17

She's worried about Buddy. We're at the Berlin Wall
and she turns to ask me if Buddy is all right. She
wants me to tell her what Buddy is feeling right
now. She wants to hear me say that he's doing fine,
he's lying down with his snout laid out on the floor
and his ears up for the tiniest noise, staring at the
door, waiting for her to walk in so that he can jump
up and run around in circles to welcome her back,
celebrating the way that only dogs do. He's perfectly
happy, I tell her. For all he knows, you might as well
be gone down the road to get a bottle of wine as off
in Berlin. Besides, he was well used to her being
away. Every time she went to New York, he stayed
with Mary, her neighbour, so he was always at home.
And whenever she came back, she would bring him
straight down to Clare so they could walk across
the Burren together, Buddy running ahead and
coming back every now and again to make sure she
was still there.

Is he OK, Liam, do you think?

He's very well looked after, Úna.

Do you think he knows?

I can't answer that. She is aware that dogs can tell what's going on, they can smell illness, but I don't want to remind her. She can be sure that Mary treats him like part of the family and he'll be even more delighted to see her when she gets back.

We're at the Berlin Wall now, what's left of it, passing along the outside with all the graffiti. Outside or inside, it's hard to know at this stage. We're looking at the height of it and saying it's not as tall as we thought, in comparison to other walls nowadays. She loves all the colour, the drawings. She gets Manfred to tell her the stories, the wall going up and families escaping, mothers handing babies across barbed wire, tunnels, spies, plus all the ironic things that happened later on when the wall came down again, like the man bringing back a library book he borrowed thirty years ago.

What were they thinking?

She asks Manfred that question like a girl. Because she likes to go back in time to the very beginning to try and work it out logically, step by step. She lets on that she's like a blank envelope and she knows nothing about the Cold War or anything to do with the twentieth century. She wants Manfred to go over the whole story again, as if that part of history was happening in front of us.

How can they put up a wall, she says, in the middle of a city? Manfred. Could you explain that to me?

So Manfred gives her a summary of the time before he was born, which is more complicated than you might think. He blows air out through his lips and gives her a list of facts while the traffic is talking over him, arguing with him. And she's ticking off things inside her head, waiting for him to come up with something new. She likes the story of the woman escaping by clinging on underneath a car, but she wants Manfred to tell her something about himself, what side of the wall he grew up on. So he tells her that he was only a child in the west and he would never have met his Polish wife, Olga, if the wall was still there.

The past is so childish, she says.

She asks Manfred would he mind getting her a bottle of water, she's thirsty. He goes away but she calls him back to give him the money. It takes a moment for her to search around in her bag, even though she can clearly see her purse from the outside. When Manfred is gone she sits forward in the wheelchair with her arms folded, trying to imagine his life.

Imagine Manfred on one side of the wall, she says, and Olga on the other, unable to get to each other. Imagine the wall coming down and Olga rushing across into Manfred's arms and they have three children in quick succession. Imagine being born at the right time, she says. Imagine being born too early or too late. Imagine not knowing that things can change. Imagine all the news not reported yet. Things we don't know yet. All the people coming after me, she says.

Imagine not knowing what happened in the past, she says. Imagine things happening and you thought they were just happening.

Imagine not knowing about 9/11.

Maybe she's lost the thread of what she was about to say. She begins worrying about Buddy again, because she once lost him on one of her walks and thought he would never come back again. It was the worst moment of her life, she says.

Don't worry about Buddy, I tell her. He's fine.

He misses me, she says.

So I try to put her mind at rest again and tell her that Buddy is the best-cared-for dog in Ireland. He's living like a prince, like a celebrity.

Manfred comes back with the water. He takes the cap off the bottle for her and she has a drink. Then she hands the bottle to me along with the cap to screw back on again and she gets out a bar of chocolate, she's hungry. I ask her would she like to go and eat something, a sandwich maybe, but she says she'll be fine with the chocolate.

I feel like a feather, she says.

She has trouble opening the chocolate. Her hands are gone weak, so I offer to help her but she snatches it away saying she can still manage.

She's dying, don't forget.

She rips the cover off the chocolate like a letter she's been waiting for. I can hear the sound of the silver paper over the traffic. She horses into it, as she would say herself, biting straight into the chocolate as if it's the last chocolate bar on earth. I can hear the black squares snapping off inside her mouth, grinding between her teeth, like she's eating bits of black tiling. She holds the bar out where she can keep an eye on it, not letting it out of her sight, waiting to break off the next bit as if she's trying to finish the whole thing before something happens, before somebody comes and takes it off her, somebody who needs it more. And she's stamping her right foot up and down. That's my memory of it, her right foot stamping on the footrest to help with the chewing. She's rocking a bit also, in a rhythm, and there is a melody, some sort of high droning note full of unspoken things coming from the back of her throat. A black paste on her lips and the noise of the traffic over the chewing. Manfred and me watching her without looking.

Sorry, she says.

Then she offers the chocolate around, speaking with a black mouth, something that doesn't sound like the full spelling.

Here, she says. I have more in my bag.

I notice that she has a big smear of chocolate across the side of her face, so I get out a tissue to clean it off. I put the tissue up to the top of the bottle of water and turn it upside down so I can wipe her face clean. She doesn't notice me doing this. Instead, she holds on to my hand and asks me again about Buddy.

Will you call Mary for me, Liam?

Now?

I need to know that he's OK, she says, has he enough water?

You want me to call her from here?

Please, Liam. He's an outdoors dog. He gets down if he doesn't get a good run.

So I make the call to Dublin, because she's getting

restless, one of those anxiety spikes. She might start crying. She's putting even larger pieces of chocolate into her mouth, two squares at a time if not more, silver paper and all, and I'm on the phone to Mary, telling her that we're making good progress, we've got as far as the Berlin Wall. We're not doing this chronologically, I explain to Mary, not the way it happened in history, more like a random tour, pick and mix. I'm on the phone saying sorry to bother you with this Mary, but there is one small problem, if that's all right, it's Buddy. I think she misses him.

I just want to say hello to him, Úna says.

So I relay that request to Mary, could she put the phone up to Buddy's ear, would that be possible? Could she put it on speaker phone maybe? And, of course, there is no question, Mary will do anything in the world. I pass the phone on to Úna so she can have a word with Buddy. She gives me what's left of the chocolate to put back into her bag while she speaks to Buddy with black teeth smiling.

Come here, Buddy, she says. Come on, good boy. You're such a good boy. There's a good boy, Buddy. Come here.

You're in Berlin.

It doesn't make sense. But you know what she's getting at, she wants him to feel that she's near. She continues slapping her hand on her thigh, saying, good boy, come here, Buddy.

He can hear me, Liam.

Manfred is standing by in case we need him.

He's barking, Liam. He knows it's me.

She hands me the phone as if I don't believe her.

Here, Liam, you speak to him.

So there I am at the Berlin Wall saying come here Buddy. Shoe, Buddy. Get the shoe. It's his favourite game. Shoe.

Stop winding him up, Úna says.

He's barking like mad now. I go through the motions, pretending to throw a shoe and hide it behind my back.

He's a Border Collie, Liam. Don't get him so worked up, he's only going to be searching all over the house, tearing the place apart, and poor Mary will have to give him a shoe of her own to calm him down again.

Shoe, Buddy. Shoe.

Will you stop tormenting him, Liam. Give me the phone.

18

He was there at the funeral, Buddy. Right up at the front, with Mary. I remember him barking once or twice in the church, everybody heard it. He must have been confused over his whereabouts. Probably thought the interior of the church was outdoors, would he? While she was dying he was very unsettled because the house was full of people coming to visit her. The house was over-subscribed, overwhelmed, one of those words. People trying to get in the door to see her, people she wanted to see and people she didn't want to see. They were all the same to Buddy, I think. What am I saying? He knows people individually, by their clothes, their smell, he knows the difference between a man and a woman. He's very intelligent, so he probably never forgets a face. And it's only a small house, a terraced cottage. Artisan, they call it. The front door opens straight onto the living room, in off the street.

He was lying on the bed with her when she died.

He must have been wondering where she was gone. Did he know it was her in the coffin, with her feet pointing away from the altar? It was a very big funeral, the church was packed. Maybe he was looking for her, among all the people there, that's what I'm thinking, that's why he barked. There was lots of singing, all the songs she had picked out herself. Buddy was well used to hearing people singing. Down in Clare. He was used to lying on the floor of a pub and hearing somebody breaking into a song and holding on to the bar counter. He probably even knew her favourite song, if that's possible, what do you think? A song in Irish. A song that she used to sing herself or say the words of, repeating the last lines again and again to herself about something that never comes again.

She didn't believe in the afterlife. There is no such thing as the next life, she said. This is the next life we're having right now, here, this minute. She said her life was no more than Buddy's life, only that she could read and write and remember the words of a song, that was all.

She didn't know why she was having a church funeral, but where else would you have it if not in a church? You end up going back to what you did your best to get away from. She always wanted to die in Dublin, by choice, like an ordinary person with a modest, heartfelt, traditional Dublin funeral, so she said. She saved up the money years ago to pay for it, because even if you believe in nothing, she said, the way Irish people did funerals gave you something to look forward to, if only you could be there yourself, in person. And she was right, I never saw so many people who were friends again in one place, under the one roof. She insisted on a full lunch for everyone in a hotel afterwards. Anyone and everybody, regardless of who said things about her and who didn't, because some people didn't like me, that's fine, some people did.

Some people really did like me, she said.

Buddy was there at the hotel as well, where else would he go? I could see him getting his bowl of food and his water like everyone else. It was a fine day, very sunny, and we were all sitting outside. I was at a table full of women, the only non-woman. They were remembering their favourite lines of poetry. So when it was my turn, I could only think of repeating the last lines from the song that she liked so much, *Trathnóna beag aréir*. That's the Irish for a small evening, last evening. What a great night we had together last night gone by and what a pity it's already turned into yesterday and never coming back. Roughly translated.

That's what I'll miss most, she says to me at the Berlin Wall. I'll miss walking with Buddy. His blurry legs running along the path. I'll miss being on the road, meeting somebody by chance. I'll miss being out in the wind, with the words taken out of your mouth, you can hardly talk.

Manfred is gone ahead to get the car and she tells me some of the things that make her happy.

People with time to spare, she says. I love people asking me questions, was I away and am I back home again. I love meeting the farmer living near Doolin, she says, the man who knows everything there is to know about Elvis, even things that Elvis never knew, the dates of all his hits, the entire discography, all the irrelevant stuff on the labels. He knows the same if not more about Chuck Berry, she says, even though you can't imagine what he needs that information for when he's out walking across the rocks. And he would never tell me this himself, she says, but I heard that he was once in the finals of *Mastermind*. He blew all his opponents away and he only fell down on some question to do with *Naked Gun*.

And Josie, the woman whose brother, Packo, died only recently, did I ever tell you that, Liam? They were such a lovely couple together, she says. I thought for years they were husband and wife, until I asked them where they found each other, was it at a dance? They laughed and said, no, we're twins. And Josie, she says, she's the only person I know who still wears one of those see-through, plastic head-scarves going to Mass. Packo never had anything to cover his head only a newspaper, you'd see him making a dash into the pub. Their friends all had names like Rosie and Peig and Jerome and Bapty, for John the Baptist.

I love meeting young people, she says. Young eyes. Young stories not made up yet. I love the young men in the Indian restaurant, talking to them about where they come from, Karachi, Nepal.

She wants to know what makes me happy.

I'm not talking about the normal things, she says, like love and drink and drugs and the day your daughter was born.

What else is there?

Things that lift your heart, Liam.

Like a lighthouse.

What lighthouse?

Any lighthouse. I tell her I feel glad whenever I
see a lighthouse. I have no idea why. Maybe it
reminds me of being close to home. Something about
the summer. Even the word lighthouse makes me
happy. I don't go looking for them. It's just lighthouses I happen to see or hear about.

You're right, she says. Lighthouses.

I tell her I'm like everyone else, I love travelling.
I love hearing languages I don't understand. Far
away languages, like Japanese. I wouldn't have a
clue what they were saying. I like that. And Irish. I
tell her I love it when *Radio na Gaeltachta* comes on
by accident in the car. When you hear somebody
talking his head off with great Irish and you don't
understand half the words.

Go mbeirimíd beo ar an ám seo arís.

She says it's the Irish for being alive around the
same time next year. Literally. May we meet again
alive this time.

19

We make a stop at a café called Einstein. I help her off with her coat, but she's still very hot and she says it feels like she has a coat on inside her. She needs to use the facilities, she calls it. I bring her as far as the ladies and help her out of the wheelchair. She can manage after that, thanks, Liam. She is able to walk without assistance, holding on to things. She closes the door behind her but doesn't lock it in case. I wait down the corridor, sort of standing guard to make sure nobody walks in on her.

I think it was mostly fathers we talked about in Café Einstein.

When she gets back to the table she is still too hot or too cold, she doesn't know the difference any more. She stands still for a moment, holding on to the table, maybe it's the pain. She sits down. She takes off the cap and everybody knows. She smiles back at them. Let them look.

She told me about her father and I told her about my father.

She orders coffee, tea for me. She wants nothing

else. She's fine with the coffee because she's already had plenty of chocolate earlier on. And when the coffee arrives along with a tiny glass of water, she drinks the water and admires the glass. She opens a sachet of sugar and ends up spilling it across the table. She gathers it all up, placing her palm on the table and pulling the grains of sugar together towards the edge. She sweeps them into the catching hand, then pours them into the coffee and slaps her hands free. She stirs the coffee and takes a sip, then sits back to look at faces. She examines all the faces available, the waitress, the people sitting opposite, two women facing each other, looking at their mobile phones.

She remembers her father's eyes. She wanted to be like her father, not like her mother. His eyes didn't care what was left behind. Her father was happier than her mother was, he loved himself more than her mother could ever love herself.

I've ordered Apfelstrudel for myself and when it arrives she leans forward to examine it. She notices that they've given me custard, even though I've asked for it without custard. It makes me think of the yellow door, that's all. It says custard on the menu, she says. Vanilla sauce, they call it, paler in colour than custard.

She picks up my fork and digs a corner off the Apfelstrudel. Then she dips the piece into the custard or vanilla sauce and puts it into her mouth, a leaf of pastry that looks a bit like soft leather with icing sugar. She nods to me and says it's lovely, how can you not like custard? And then she continues eating as if she's ordered it for herself. Until it's nearly half gone, then she puts down the fork and leaves the rest.

Úna. You've eaten half of it.

She laughs. Sorry.

You might as well finish it now, I tell her.

Don't give me any more, she says. She pushes the plate away and looks at the two women sitting across from us, travelling together. One of the women is now leafing through a guide book trying to decide where they want to go next. The other woman holds a camera in her hands, probably going back over the photographs of where they have already been.

My father's eyes had the city and the country in them, Úna says.

She tells me that her father made all the connections between people and towns. He knew where they were from and what brought them to the city. His eyes understood what they owned and what they wanted and what they had lost. He collected all the talking and the noise and the smell of smoke and beer in their clothes. What people said when they were squashed together at the bar counter. She remembers the bar in Dublin where he often went. It had a phone box in it so you could close the door and keep out the noise while you called home to say you were held up.

She's opening another sachet of sugar. Or not. She is flapping it back and forth in preparation without actually doing so.

Her father's eyes kept everything they saw. Her mother's eyes denied everything they saw. My father's eyes kept all the occasions, she says, the celebrity weddings and the public functions in the Mansion House. All the black-and-white photographs of Dublin in the sixties, people drinking wine they were not used to yet in Ireland. People smiling a lot. People self-conscious and not aware of what they owned yet. When having no money was not such a bad thing as it is now, because people really had no money then, only an account in the grocery shops. When things were getting better than before. It was a time, she says, when you had dance halls and function rooms full of smoke and sweat and perfume in the air. Men in bow ties and women with off-the-shoulder dresses and holy medals well hidden. People being continental, looking rich, behaving modern, even though it was still Dublin and everybody knew everyone else, she says, everyone knew what you had or didn't have. So it was not possible to be anonymous.

Anything that was not worth seeing through her father's eyes was not worth happening. Because it was his job as a journalist to know what receptions were worth attending and who was worth talking about and what was worth remembering. What politicians liked to be seen in the company of women who were still women. When times were glamorous like they never were before in Ireland, she says, when it was glamorous to be an air hostess, when it was glamorous to be a journalist, glamorous even to be a priest. A time before avocadoes. A time before yoghurt. A time before toasted ham-and-cheese sandwiches, even.

Her father wrote about it all, she says. All the people busy catching up with the future. People not letting on where they came from. When the taste of freedom was new and the history of Ireland was only just gone by. When the country was smaller than it seems now, she says, more compact, more innocent. When the only colour in the streets was the golden glow of the pubs, she says. When it was customary to sing in maternity wards and you'd see empty bottles of Guinness rolling under the new mother's bed. When divorce was not a word and going to London was the saying for expecting a baby and a baby not born yet was more alive than the mother. When being a woman was the word for not being a man. When going abroad was the word for Europe. When Ireland was still far away, full of scenery and flag days and motorcades and hurling finals and signs painted on granite walls by the sea, reminding swimmers that togs must be worn. Conversations full of men only and pink male bodies coming out of the cold sea.

And togs well worn, she says.

Her father brought her with him to the horse fair in Smithfield, she says. She can remember sitting in the back of the car, looking at his eyes in the mirror. I wanted to keep his eyes, she says, and be a man. I wanted to be the driver of a car, smoking out the window and looking back in the mirror. I wanted to be a woman like a man. A woman with the viewpoint of a man. A man only a woman, in a women-only way. I admired him as a small girl of six would, she says, the confidence in him, like a packet of cigarettes gave you confidence and the person who owned a packet of cigarettes owned the world. I remember everything, she says, the people coming up to shake his hand, offering him a cigarette, a drink, inducements of friendship. I remember people handing over their life stories like they were giving away everything precious they had inherited. People eager and shy, wiping their hands on their trousers before they shook his, because they may have touched a horse or a cow or a shovel before him. Women with flour on their hands clapping.

He wore the city in his suit, she says. He carried the power of words before it was called the media.

She can remember the men at the horse fair showing the horses how to smile. Her father was laughing with a woman who was not her mother. And the woman who was not her mother smiling like the horses. And then a boy on a runaway horse came racing through the crowd. He could not be stopped, so the woman who was not her mother grabbed her hand and everyone had to scatter with their backs against the wall of the pub. And she spilled the red lemonade on her dress.

She says the woman who was not her mother started coming to the house. I remember them arguing over dinner together, she says, around the table, my father and my mother and the woman who was not my mother. The woman who was not my mother got up over something that was said by my mother and walked straight out the door, with my father after her and my mother after him. That's how I remember it, she says. We didn't have the words to describe what was happening in our own family. We were children watching. None of us could understand any of it. It was like seeing your own legs in the water when you go swimming and you wonder if they still are your own legs, she says. Because it was only years later that she understood what was going on around the table, how the woman who was not her mother had come to ask her father to go to Australia with her. She wanted to buy my father from my mother, she says. She had the money to do that. She wanted my father to leave us all behind and go off to Australia, she says, with no children.

So then, she says, her mother must have said something. She put up a fuss and said nobody was going anywhere. Nobody was leaving until they were finished eating. The least they could do was appreciate the food that she had cooked for them. She had put all the love she had left into that dinner and she started drinking wine very fast, in big gulps, she says, because my father was thinking of leaving us all and going to Australia. Her father got up and said he had enough, he was not hungry. The woman who was not her mother got up and ran after him, out the door. We stood at the window watching them all, she says, marching away after each other, down the street. My mother fell and we saw her left in a heap on the ground.

20

The two women sitting at the table opposite in Café Einstein look over at us. They look as if they feel they've been looked at. We look back at them. Then we all look away in different directions, as if we're taking no notice of each other. The waitress comes to our table and picks up the empty plate. She asks if there is anything else we might need, more water maybe.

It's lovely water, Úna says to the waitress. Is it tap water, just?

Yes, the waitress says. It's ordinary tap water.

Úna says she started out trying to make sure she was not like her mother. She says she ended up being like her father. Or was it the other way round? Back and forth. I went to London, she says, to try and be myself. But the more I was myself the more I was like them.

It felt like they were coming after me, everywhere I went, I couldn't get away. I remember them sending my brother over to London. My father sent him because he didn't want to be responsible for his own son any more. He didn't want his own son loitering around Dublin, getting into trouble, bringing his good name into disrepute. Because he was the king, she says, the king of journalism, the king of the city and all the people gathered at receptions. He didn't want his son to be his weakness. He didn't want to be reminded of his role as a father and having to love his own son. He wanted his son out of sight, out of harm, so he sent him to London for me to look after. Jimmy, she says, he was not even eighteen. He was only a boy and I should have done more for him.

She says she loved her brother so much she was afraid of him. He was our Don Carlos, she says, killed by his own father, sending him off to London with no love in him.

He was the baby in the family, she says. Curly hair and big open eyes, like his father. I was already in secondary school when he was born, she says, so I remember him sitting on my knee and I knew what it was like to be his mother. I put his shoes on and taught him how to tie his laces. I put stories into his head and heard them coming back through his imagination, everything repeated. I remember him sleepy after waking up, trying to make him laugh. You could never be angry with him. He followed me around the house, watching everything I was doing, asking me why was I drawing over my eyebrows with a pencil and where was I going and what was in the book I was reading. Not letting me out of his sight. He was there every morning, waiting for me to get up because his mother was still passed out from drinking the night before.

113

He was a child unable to grow up. He was like his father, good at being out in pubs with people around him. Like his mother, good at holding the drink and not opening his eyes. I could see him already ending up like his mother and father and maybe that's what made me so afraid of him, his weakness.

My brother, my weakness, she says.

He stayed a few nights with me in London, she says, he slept on the floor. She went to work and he was there when she came home, waiting for her. He had that look in his eyes that says will you tell me what to do, will you show me where to go. He hardly had the confidence to fill in a form or make a phone call. He missed appointments and left things behind, lost money out of his pocket, she says. He thought everybody in London was like a big family. He expected the world to be his friend, just as he wanted his mother to be his mother, just as he wanted his father to be his father and not send him away over to London where he was on his own.

She says she was only finding her feet at the time. Do you understand me, Liam? I didn't even know how to be my own friend. I gave my brother money but he had no idea how to hold on to it and came back looking for more. I told him he couldn't be expecting me to be his mother and father for him, she says, he just had to get used to being on his own like everyone else.

Liam, she says, he looked into my eyes but I couldn't let him in.

She says she remembered his birthday. Even if I

got it wrong by a few days, she says, or a week. If there was ever a time I missed his birthday it was because he went missing and I couldn't find him. I swear to God, Liam, I always remembered his birthday, like a big sister.

She picks up the napkin and holds it in her hand. She folds it up and then unfolds it again, not lifting it up to her eyes.

21

Her hands are swollen. She begins to search around in her bag and finds some hand cream that I didn't know she had, maybe it was hidden by other things. She takes the lid off the tub and puts some of the cream on her hands. The smell of hand cream is like custard, vanilla sauce.

She wants to know more about my childhood but I have nothing much to tell her. All I remember is being out fishing and my father pulling on the oars and the water dripping from the oars. I remember honey dripping from the spoon at the breakfast table and my father twisting the spoon around quickly to stop the honey running. I remember the water hammering in the pipes at night and the mice running along the floor.

You must remember more than that, she says.

I tell her I've forgotten everything and my brother's memory is far better than mine. I always wanted to put things behind me as fast as possible and I left it up to him to remember. He keeps everything in his head so I can forget. Dates, times, places, all the details of what happened. His memory is the same as mine, no difference, only that he knows where to find it.

That's absurd, she says.

She doesn't believe it's possible for me to have so few personal memories. I must be suppressing things. I tell her my memory is unreliable. That's not the word that I wanted to use, unreliable, not to be trusted. Resistant, recalcitrant, some word like that.

I'm only suppressing things I can't remember.

She closes up the tub of hand cream and puts it back into her bag. Then she leans forward to let me know something. She says she once read about a writer who said you were always crawling towards the truth. Which is true, she says. She came from a time that was only crawling towards the truth and she couldn't wait that long, she had to speak out. It's all in my books, she says. I didn't make it look beautiful. I didn't make it look worse, or better. It was the honesty I was after, nothing else.

The rhythm of honesty, she calls it.

She's afraid I have no rhythm.

She says I need to bring everything out into the open. I can't be like an empty field any more with nothing built on it, it's impossible to be alive without remembering.

Tell me about your father, she says.

So then I try to get into the rhythm, in Café Einstein. She's a good listener and she gives me time to explain.

We were far too honest, I tell her. That was our

117

problem, too much honesty. My father was a school-teacher, I explain to her, so he had a good method for finding out what was going on inside your head. He cross-examined me and my brother separately, so we could never agree on a story together. The details were always a bit off. I was the reflection of my older brother, but we sometimes remembered things differently. We were easily confused, always caught out.

My father was trying to find out the truth, I tell her.

About what?

The Jesuit. My uncle, the Jesuit.

It was the silence, I explain to her. My father's brother made our family very silent. We thought it was good to be silent. We were all trying to be as silent as a Jesuit and get away with saying nothing, so nobody could guess what was inside our heads. We used to go out to the field and play hurling, just the two of us, my brother and me, whacking the ball to each other, back and forth. I still remember the sound of the wood against the leather ball. I remember him catching the ball, taking it out of the air with his hand like you would pick an apple. A stinging apple. Then he would swing his body around and send the ball back. That's all we did for hours, like a conversation with only one word. We were so honest, myself and my brother, we only said the most necessary things to each other. I think we were being exactly like my father and his brother, as silent as possible. They had nothing to say to each other apart from talking about world events, history, the economy. Me and my brother had nothing to say to each other either, nothing that ever connected up into a conversation. Only the essential practicalities, that's all. And facts. A few bits of general information that we were trying to get right for my father, facts like highest mountains, largest lakes, longest roads, things you learn in school basically.

We went up a mountain together once without saying much for a whole day. We were afraid to talk about seeing my father's brother coming out of the hotel in Cork with my aunt. We didn't even want to admit that we were in Cork at the same time. We didn't want to tell each other that my aunt and my father's brother were cousins. The less we knew the less could be extracted under pressure. Anything you say to yourself you end up saying out loud in the end, I knew that, so we pretended we didn't carry any of that information with us.

The sound at Café Einstein keeps renewing itself. Cups and plates and pots of coffee clicking as they are being set out on the tables. She's listening to everything I'm saying. Then she finds some lip balm that I didn't know she had in her bag either. Where did all these things come from? Her lips are very dry. She's dehydrated, even though she's been drinking lots of water.

We were on a fishing holiday, I explain to her. Staying in a hotel right next to a lake. The lake was called Lough Conn. And out through the windows of the hotel we could see a mountain called Nephin.

The mountain was asking to be climbed. Every morning it was there at breakfast like a challenge.

So one day my father allowed us to climb the mountain, me and my brother, we were only about thirteen and fourteen at the time. We had sandwiches and soft drinks in a rucksack each, identical. We set off from the hotel with the lake behind us and the mountain rising up ahead. The cattle were chewing. There were rushes in the fields, like eyebrows. Fuchsia hedges along the side of the road with a line of bright red dust underneath. I can clearly remember a tractor passing by, followed by a dog, followed by the smell of diesel. The man on the tractor raised his hand without looking back. And the mountain came back into view every now and then, a big surprise around the next bend, closer and larger than before.

All these things I remember, but we never spoke about them, we didn't trust each other.

It was like a silent country we were walking through. We cut in off the road where the fields came to an end and the bog took over. The bog was covered in heather, like a complicated softness under my feet. I felt the breeze in my armpits. The fields were shrinking behind us and there was nobody around, no other witnesses. About halfway up the mountain, we sat down and had our sandwiches. The lake looked more stretched out, more like a piece of blue tiling, reflected. We lay back for a while staring at the clouds moving across the sky above us. Every time the sun went in it was like the end of the day and every time the sun came out again was like a new day beginning. Sometimes it looked like the clouds had come to a standstill and we were forced to believe that the mountain was carrying us away.

And then my brother spoke to me. He talked about the Jesuit and said it was better for us to agree on a plan. So we made an official agreement to remain silent. We agreed to be as silent as my father and my father's brother and not speak a word about having chips or staying in the hotel in Cork and seeing my father's brother with my aunt, two cousins holding hands.

I remember getting up and telling my brother we better carry on before it started raining. He told me to go ahead, he would catch up. So I kept going and left my brother behind me. Every once in a while I looked back down and he was still there, lying on his back looking at the clouds taking him further and further away. I remember the strong wind and the rocks where the heather stopped growing and the small cairn at the summit. The view was gone, the rain came down, I was inside a cloud.

My brother disappeared. When I got back down again I looked for him. I called him. Maybe I came down in a different place, so I thought at the time, where he was not to be found. So I had to carry on back to the hotel on my own, without my brother. I was worried what my father might ask him to say, so I hurried along the same road back to the lake to try and catch up with him, past the cattle bunched together in the corner of a field, past the same rushes dripping and the sound of water left running. I kept thinking of my brother walking only yards ahead of me, but I was mistaken.

I was the first to get to the hotel and it was my brother who was still missing. My father questioned me, but I only gave him the most necessary information, that myself and my brother split up, that's all. I told him that I went up to the top of the mountain and then it started raining, we lost each other. My father said it was very irresponsible to split up like that and my mother told him to wait until my brother came back before he said any more.

We were all staring around the room waiting. There were photographs of the lake and the mountain everywhere, to remind you of the real lake and the real mountain outside. And fishing. No matter where you went, in the corridors, the bedrooms, you couldn't get away from men holding up a salmon or a lake trout, hanging their catch on the weighing scales. Men in boats, men in oilskins, men smiling and raising a glass of whiskey afterwards. Famous men who had come to the hotel, lucky enough to catch a fish while they were there. And flies for sale at the reception. Thousands of beautiful flies in colours that you could never believe, nothing you could ever imagine seeing in real life. They had workshops for people learning how to tie mayflies with bits of chicken feathers and deer hair and I knew I would be very good at that kind of thing if I let myself. The biggest pike ever caught on the lake was in a glass case over the bar, with his mouth open, serrated teeth. And beside him, the coloured fly on a hook that he had been caught by.

It was getting late and my mother was even more worried standing up than she was sitting down. She wanted to call the rescue services because it was nearly dark. And then my brother walked in the door.

He has decided to come back, my father said.

My mother ran to embrace my brother and the front of her dress got soaked. My father was even more angry at seeing him back safe again, so after my mother changed my brother's clothes and dried his hair with a towel and sang a song to calm him down, my father asked him for a full explanation. My brother told him that he followed me up to the top of the mountain and I was gone. My mother tried to intervene, but my father told her to keep out of it, she had not been on the mountain, so she had nothing to say. My brother said it started raining and I said it started raining and my father said he couldn't believe either of us.

And what happened then?

My brother gave in. I think he was trying to save me from getting punished. He told my father about my aunt giving us fish and chips in Cork. How the car was left on a hill and somebody who knew how to drive had to come and point it in the right direction again. My brother explained how we stayed in a hotel for the night and we were not tired, so we got dressed and went downstairs to explore without permission. We didn't do anything, my brother said. We were only there by accident when my aunt came out of the hotel with my father's brother. We were standing at the railings minding our own business, he said. He told my father everything, the smile my aunt had in her eyes, full of sadness and happiness.

123

How she went arm in arm with my father's brother, and he was wearing a light-grey suit, like an ordinary man, not a Jesuit.

My mother began to cry.

My father said he was glad the truth had been told, finally.

My mother cried and said now she knew why my father's brother, the Jesuit, was no longer coming to our house to visit.

Instead of punishing us, my father came over to embrace me. He held my head sideways against his chest, so I could feel the sharp point of a pencil in his top pocket against my face. He embraced me for a long time and I wanted to escape. The pencil was sticking deeper into my face the more he loved me. I was more afraid of his love than I was of his anger. His love and his anger were nearly the same, no difference, full of things that could not be put right in his family, lots of cruel reasons and lonely times he spent as a boy in West Cork without a father. It made him press my face harder and harder against his chest. He would not let go, possibly for two minutes, maybe three or four. When he finally let go, he turned to my brother and embraced him in the same way, for the same duration, to make sure he loved us both equally, no difference.

We kept our memories separate after that. My brother and me. Just like my father and my father's brother. We were like counterspies in the same house, sitting at the same breakfast table and passing each other by on the stairs.

Maybe I should be talking to your brother, she says.

I don't have his memory, Úna.

You did too many drugs, Liam.

No. It's not that.

I tell her it has nothing to do with drugs or not being able to remember. It's got to do with who owns that memory, me or my brother. He wanted to keep that story of the mountain. Like he kept the story of my aunt and the Jesuit arm in arm. Please, he was always saying, let me remember the mountain story. So I gave it to him. I decided to let him keep it. I told him it belonged to him and he didn't have to worry, I was not going to take it back off him or tell anyone it was mine.

22

As we were coming out of Café Einstein the waitress came running after us. Manfred was helping Úna into the car and she was already sitting down putting her seat belt on when we looked around and saw the waitress standing by on the pavement with the money in her hand.

This is not right, the waitress was saying.

It was embarrassing with all the people passing along street and the waitress calling – Hallo, excuse me, this is not right. There must be some mistake. Even though it was not the mistake you would expect, not what the people watching would have thought when they saw the waitress with the money in one hand and the restaurant bill in the other. It was the opposite. The truth of the matter was that the tip Úna left behind on the table was so enormous, there had to be some kind of mistake.

She smiled at the waitress and told her to keep it. It was no mistake, because she knew what it was like to be a waitress, she knew what the money was like to receive, more than what it was to give.

Put that away now, she said. You keep that for yourself.

She said it like an aunt. Like a mother. Even though the waitress continued saying it was a mistake, she could not accept it, please, take it back, it's far too much. I remember the waitress closing her fist on the money and holding it up against her chest, in tears, because I think she knew the money was being transferred from a dying person to a living person. She stood on the pavement waving goodbye.

23

Then she's asleep.

Your mother is asleep, Manfred says. Will I stop the car?

I ask her would she like to lie down. Would you like to go back to the hotel and lie down for a while? But she doesn't answer. Her eyes are closed and she doesn't hear me.

I tell Manfred to keep going.

Where?

Anywhere, just keep driving.

The back of her head is rolling from side to side, lolling, if you prefer. Until the side of her forehead comes to rest against the frame of the car. The bag has slipped from her grasp. I just about catch it before the contents spill out and put it on the seat beside her. I place her hands in her lap, one across the other, palms up. Her mouth is open, she could be dead.

She's asleep with all the architecture going by. All the streets that she's missing. Look at all the people passing us by, I want to say to her. All the things I'm seeing for her, with my own eyes, while she's asleep. Like what? Houses. Shops. Traffic. Overhead trains. A whole city slipping by, street by street. All the graffiti on the walls and the doors and shops and train stations. Graffiti up high where people don't go. Graffiti on trees. Graffiti on people. Graffiti on the plinth of a horse rider, an oversized nobleman still on his horse with the weeds growing around him. Riding through the city weeds. Riding past the people. And the people riding past him on their bikes, in every direction. Layers of memory over memory over shops over banks over schools over courthouses and galleries and everything that moves.

What else?

If she wasn't asleep I would tell her to look at the two men embracing outside a train station, kissing each other cheek by cheek five times before they part and one goes down the steps and the other walks away along the street. I want to tell her about the man I see waiting for another man to finish the bottle he's drinking so he can have it to add to all the other bottles he's collecting in a blue Ikea bag on his shoulder. I want to tell her I saw a man checking the contents of the street bin with a small flashlight. I saw a woman with two children on her bike, front and back, talking to them both as she's passing by. Also. An old man with a ponytail sitting outside a café with a red rug over his knees. Also. A man wearing a white apron and a white cap on his head, smoking a cigarette outside a restaurant, with white flour on his hands and face. Also. A father and daughter crossing the street. He's wearing a leather jacket with *psychobilly* written on it. You'd hardly know they were father and daughter, more like brother and sister maybe. Only that they're holding hands and she looks like him. I have no idea what they could be talking about, maybe something to do with a dog. That's what I'm guessing. I think she's asking him if they can get a dog.

Maybe the people are like the city they live in, I'm thinking, or is it the other way around, the city is like the people that live there. Úna would have something to say about that, I'm sure, but she's asleep and we're driving around in circles with her mouth open.

I get talking to Manfred. I ask him general questions. Who else does he normally drive around the city? He speaks over his shoulder and tells me he drives around men in suits mostly. He never likes asking them what they're up to, unless they tell him. It's not his business. It's not his car. He's only the driver and the fleet belongs to his cousin.

Manfred tells me about an American hip-hop artist he collected from the airport recently. He gives me the name but I've never heard of him before. The hip-hop artist apologized for not speaking German, Manfred says, then he kept talking all the way from the airport to the hotel, in English. He had a strong American accent which Manfred could not understand very well, it had such a fast rhythm and it was hard for him to stop the flow. Manfred says he had a red beard and he wore the clothes of his sister. If he had a sister, Manfred says. A light-blue jumper with a diagonal pattern of rabbits and lightning strikes. Blue lightning strikes, he says, across the chest. He was also wearing green shorts and luminous green socks, up to his knees.

I checked him out afterwards on the net, that's how I remember the green socks and the green shorts.

Manfred tells me that he brought the hip-hop artist to the venue and that he was invited to stay for the performance, so that he could bring him back to his hotel afterwards, very late. The venue was packed, so Manfred is saying. The hip-hop artist had a huge fan base and the place was full of people dancing and crashing into each other. It was very loud, you would have to wear earplugs. Manfred says he's not accustomed to that volume any more. My ears were whistling for two days, he says. Crazy. I couldn't hear my own television. There are two drummers in the band, he says, the rest is mostly technology, and there is a large green skull over the stage which keeps lighting on and off to the music. When the lights go off, Manfred says, the green skull is flying high over the crowd. The green skull flickering on and off very rapidly to the beat. The green skull man. Or was it the skull of a green woman? Who knows? He has no body but he has a life, Manfred says, with the music.

Manfred tells me that he's a family man now. And when you have children, he says, you forget how important all that clubbing scene is. It's good to know that it's all still there, he says, within reach, without you, all those things he might or might not have done before, without going into the details. While Manfred is talking I get the feeling that I've been in the wrong place up to now. I should have been here in this city from the start. I've been missing something. Like music I was not aware of and should have been listening to if I wasn't already listening to something else. I should be here, where everything is available. Everything is in your grasp, so I thought to myself.

This city doesn't mind what age you are, Manfred says.

And as we're stopped briefly at traffic lights again, I'm looking out at some people sitting on a bench. It seems to me that it's a grandfather and a father and a son. Three generations. You can tell, they look very alike, only different ages, that's all. Three different stages of the same man, you could say. The father is talking to the grandfather, telling a story, using his hands. The grandfather has some beads in his hand and he's listening to his son telling the story, while his grandson is playing with a piece of blue twine. The boy begins tying the blue twine around his grandfather's head. The grandfather hardly notices the twine going around his own head because he's listening. The father keeps talking, occasionally elbowing the boy, telling him to stop doing that to his grandfather. But the boy ignores him, because his father and his grandfather are so deeply involved in the conversation that they are not really bothered by the thin blue twine going around the grandfather's chin, around the ears, up over his bald head and back down under the chin again. The father continues telling the story and the grandfather continues listening and the boy continues tying the blue twine around the grandfather's head. That's all I saw. We moved on, so I didn't find out what happened after that.

24

She wakes up. She makes a barking sound at the back of her throat and looks out the window to see where she is.

Was I asleep with my mouth open?

No, I say.

Liam, you're such a liar, she says. I hate that, sleeping with my mouth open.

It's as though she has the ability to remember everything that's been said while she was asleep. Because she tells me to grow up, my clubbing days are over. Be yourself, she says, there are plenty of other things in the city apart from the night-life. And then I'm thinking that maybe she was not asleep at all, only sitting with her head back like a listening device, picking up everything myself and Manfred were talking about, including the green skull.

And then we have an emergency in the car, her feet were causing trouble, so I remember.

Liam, I can't feel my feet. My feet don't belong to me any more. They're not my feet, Liam. Could that be right? My feet don't feel like my feet any more, she said.

Is it the medication? Is it her circulation? Would she like to go back to the hotel now? No, she says, keep going, because there's nothing much to do back in the hotel room and she doesn't want to sit in the foyer of the Adlon listening to piano music all day, whether it's a real piano player or just a piano playing of its own accord, doesn't matter. It's only her feet, they feel so tight, squeezed into her shoes. The best thing for me to do in that case is to raise her legs up onto the seat, so she's travelling sideways.

Free the feet, she says.

I loosen the laces and pull her shoes off by the heel. I put the socks into her bag and then she wants her toenails cut.

Look at them, she says. They're too long. They're jamming up against the tips of my shoes.

Fair enough.

They're cutting into my toes, Liam.

We're going to be late for a lunch meeting, but what does that matter?

This has nothing to do with time-keeping, it has to do with now, here and now. So I ask Manfred if he could do us a favour and stop so we can get a pair of nail clippers. What would be the best place around here, without going too much out of the way? So Manfred tells us not to worry, it's probably best for him to park somewhere and go out himself to get the nail clippers. She says thanks Manfred, this is very kind of you. Make sure it's a good pair

135

of nail clippers, she says, proper industrial ones, not those cheap ones that go sideways and slip out of your fingers and don't even cut the nail only score it with a little mark before it breaks. Manfred knows exactly what she's talking about.

I understand, he says, big nail clippers for the feet.

25

Manfred disappears. We're watching the street corner where he went out of sight, waiting for him to come back with the nail clippers. Another man appears and it takes a moment for us to realize that it's not Manfred, until he walks right past ignoring us. We go back to waiting for Manfred.

I want to ask her something about Milltown Malbay. The singer she told me about, holding on to the bar counter. During the music festival, with the pub so crawling with people that nobody could move in or out the door. Was he wearing a blue suit jacket? Did he have a black T-shirt underneath?

Yes, she says. I think so.

Did he have the other hand on his hip?

Yes, I think so.

Had he got his eyes closed? Had he got his chest out and his shoulders back? Because that's the way I remember it, the man singing in the crowded bar in Milltown Malbay, he had his eyes open just once, very briefly, to look at something over the door. Even though there was nothing up there to look at and he was only doing so to remember the words, then he closed his eyes again.

He had a voice like a new car, I remember. She agrees with that. He sang a song called *A stór mo chroí*, my heart's love. We agree on that as well. We also agree that he was not a famous singer, not professional. He never made a recording. He only became a singer at that very moment, as he began to sing. It was the song that turned him into a singer, as soon as people called for silence. So that was his only recording, the people listening. We were his recording. He was our recording, because we were there at the same time, myself and Emily, listening to the man with his eyes closed and a voice like a new car singing.

I tell her about a time I was trying to go back to Milltown Malbay. Around the time that my daughter was born. I couldn't believe what was in my grasp, holding the baby's head, looking at her eyes opening, the tiny fingers, the cry, quivering. You could say I was astonished at the idea of being a father, excited, exhilarated, all those words that don't really explain anything. I was delirious, no other word for it. I had the feeling that I was escaping from myself, that for once, nobody was following me.

When she was only two weeks old, it was discovered that the baby had a cyst on one of her breasts. Something she was born with, I would never have noticed it myself. A tiny growth that seemed completely harmless but could have turned malignant. The paediatricians were telling us it would be a matter of concern, if it was not removed right away, surgically. She was only two weeks old and she was having to go for an operation, under general anaesthetic. They said it would leave no more than a small scar, but all the same. It was more serious than we thought. I kept reassuring Emily that it was nothing. The baby would not even remember it. No. That's not true. Of course I knew it had to be a total nightmare and the baby would feel abandoned. Only there was nothing we could do, that's what I was saying, the operation had to proceed and we could not be present in theatre.

Emily was asked to provide some breast milk. So she got a breast pump and filled a lot of sterilized jars full of her milk and brought them in to be labelled and kept in storage. The baby's name was written on all the jars, my surname.

We were only just getting used to calling her Maeve.

So there we stood on the street outside the hospital not knowing what to do, we felt so alone without the baby. Emily kept looking up at the windows. I have no idea what she was hoping to see. Medical staff dressed in green gowns and green masks over their faces. I had to pull her away down the street by the arm and we sat in a café with nothing to say, not even looking into each other's eyes, not drinking the coffee or eating the scones we ordered either, only me talking and her not listening, as if she couldn't hear me.

Emily kept repeating the baby's name, trying to feel close to her. Maeve. Maeveen. She kept wanting to find out if there was any news yet, but there was nothing we could possibly do only wait.

And the thing was this, I was mad about her. I loved Emily in a way that you can only love a mother after having a baby. I was ready to do anything in the world to distract her and make her happy. So I got her into the car and started driving, just to stop her worrying about what the baby was going through. I don't know what came over me only that I felt I had to take action, go somewhere, get away from what was making her so sad, she had all this milk love in her breasts. I know this sounds crazy and it is, but all I could think of doing at the time was to keep driving through the streets, any direction. I had the music on and the windows open, it was absurd. I kept talking, saying anything at all that might cheer her up and make her smile again.

Remember the bar with the bathroom at the back, I kept saying to Emily. Where you had to go through the kitchen, through the smell of soup and washing-up liquid and tea leaves. Emily, remember us when we were escaping, you were sitting on the edge of the bath with the enamel all cracked, a million hair-line cracks. Because that's what happens when you pour boiling water into old baths like that, the enamel begins to crack into tiny surface fractures, no real harm done, only that it makes the bath look even older than it is. A bath with wrinkles, that's what Emily called it back then. I reminded her how we laughed about it, wondering how many people must have had a bath in it over the years. How many generations of mothers and fathers and grand-mothers and grandfathers would fit together in a bath like that with the water up to their ears? And how many children lay back and put their heads down, only their noses and their eyes up over the surface, looking at the steamed-up tiles, listening to the world with all the sound gone under, the pipework clicking and the overflow plughole slurping and the underwater sounds coming from the bar, the empty glasses being collected and the voice of a singer like an engine humming and a lot of swallowing.

I'm just driving. Driving with this thing stuck in my head, something I want to re-create which has nothing to do with what's happening right now in our lives. Emily is sitting beside me, asking me where we're going and I'm not listening to her. I keep on driving and wondering what it would be like to go back, if the cracked bath is still there at all any more, or has it been replaced. I imagine it like a re-enactment. Emily and me going into that bar in Milltown Malbay, sitting down for a drink together. And after a while she gets up to go to the bathroom, because the men's toilets are out in the yard, so it's up to her to check. I wait for her in the bar, looking around to see how much I remember. For a place that was so full of people the last time we were there, it seems very empty now, only the barman stacking bottles. Then she comes back out to the bar and sits down beside me, smiling. Yes, Liam, she says. The bath is still there, with all the cracks left in it. And the hot water boiler above. And the two green lines. And the chain with the stopper gone grey.

That's how I imagined it. Everything the same as

it was. The road to the coast. The seaweed baths, the Pollock Holes, the sky, the rocks, the empty landscape, all intact. The entire shoreline unchanged.

There is no way of explaining this, even talking about it feels like waking up on the edge of the cliffs, opening my eyes and staring down at the way I was then. I was obsessed with making up a story for myself. My imagination was more real than my life.

I mean, this is the mother of a two-week-old baby in hospital. Emily was still very pale after the birth. It showed up her freckles. The milk love in her breasts was leaking all over the car so I brought her straight back to the hospital. She was crying and she left the car door open. She ran, or half-ran, that's how I remember it, in through the revolving doors. I saw her turning right, then left, then right again before she disappeared. I parked the car and went in after her and it was as if she couldn't recognize me, as if I was not even the father and she could not speak to me until she was told that the operation was over, the baby was fine, sleeping now. She asked if she could sit beside the cot.

26

Manfred gets back. I see him appearing around the corner but I don't actually believe it's him until he comes right up to the car and smiles in through the window. He opens the door and hands me a small white plastic bag with the nail clippers. He apologizes for taking so long, but Úna tells him it's fine, we were having a chat and we didn't even notice him gone.

The nail clippers come in a plastic wrapper and it takes me ages, you know those sealed packages that are almost impossible to open up without mutilating yourself. I have to tear away at the cardboard backing. She's waiting patiently and then I finally manage to wrench the nail clippers out. We're ready to begin. The big pedicure, I say to her. I put my jacket on my knees and lift her feet up. We can't rush this, I'm telling myself. It's a delicate thing. I ask Manfred to wait, because we can't be driving and cutting toenails at the same time.

I can be good at this. I start with the big toe and work my way down to the little toe. I just concentrate on what I'm doing and she watches me. She starts telling me something about Bob Dylan, did I know that you can look at the entire double album being played on the internet now.

No, I say, not looking up.

I come from a time of vinyl, she says. And vinyl is making a comeback. At least you can see the double album being played again, she says. A pair of hands brings out each disk and lays it down on the turntable. The disk begins to spin and the needle touches down with a scrape and a hiss, the way it used to. Imagine, she says. You can listen to the whole thing and watch the printed information on the centre label rotating. Columbia, she says. All the crackles underneath the songs, completely authentic.

I offer to play it for her on my phone, but she doesn't want that, she doesn't have the attention span now.

When I'm finished doing her toenails I gather up the bits and put them into the paper bag that came with the toenail clippers. I put the clippers into her see-through bag and I put the bag with the cut-off toenails into my jacket pocket. She says her feet are quite itchy and hot, so I rub some hand cream on them. The sensation has come back into her feet and she starts laughing, it tickles. She's laughing and coughing, so I have to stop. I tell Manfred to go ahead, he can drive on. I open the windows to cool her feet and she stretches out her toes, wriggling them in the breeze. Then I put her shoes and socks back on.

Thanks, Liam.

There you are now. How does that feel?

My feet are my own again, she says.

I tie the shoelaces and one of them breaks, so I put the broken piece of white shoestring into my jacket pocket as well. Where else do you put these things?

27

I had no idea how to be a father. I was completely unprepared when the baby came out of hospital. I thought things would just fall into place. I was like a boy on a bike. There's no other way of describing it. A boy freewheeling through the puddles with my legs out.

I think she rescued me. Maeve. Maeveen.

There was a fire at the house where we had been living. It was not fit for a baby any more, never was. Emily and myself had a flat in a terraced house where people had a lot of parties. Spontaneous parties that erupted late and sometimes went on till lunchtime the next day, all kinds of stuff being taken. Bottles left on the stairs. It was that type of place, there was a great turnover of faces, you hardly got to know anybody properly. We had a great time, it has to be said, and it would be misleading to give the impression it wasn't me and Emily throwing most of the parties ourselves, but now we had moved on to the family stage.

I thought the baby would be fine there for a while,

we made it nice. I should have planned something better, but to be honest, I had no money and I was not very good at making plans, only planning to get out of things, planning to get away from my father, for example, away from home. I got used to living unprepared, with people coming and going through my life. I was doing what I thought everyone else in Ireland was doing at the time, planning to have no plans, hoping everything would look after itself, and if not, you could always leave it behind and go away, abroad. And then there was a fire downstairs one day, somebody careless with a cigarette or a candle, it was bound to happen. We came back to find the front door open and water all over the hallway. There was some half-burned furniture and curtains thrown into the front garden. The banisters were charred, you could see where the flames had begun to bite into the paint, dark teeth-marks in the wood. The walls were blackened with smoke along the stairs. Our rooms had been broken into by the fire officers in order to secure the building, they had opened all the windows. I can still remember the smell of dampness and burned wood. It was in our clothes, in the books, in everything we owned, even the electrical equipment. A sharp smell of things half-eaten, coughed up by fire.

How could you bring a baby back there?

What was I thinking? We had to find somewhere to stay for the night. So I brought Emily and the baby to the only place I knew. Not far from where I grew up. There were some guesthouses along the seafront that I remembered from when I used to go swimming as a boy. It was the only thing that came to mind. I couldn't go home, for all the obvious reasons. And for somebody who was so keen on getting away from home, it's strange to think I came up with nothing better than getting accommodation so close to home, back to where I started.

It was me and Emily and the baby, the three of us together. We were on our own now. And I had the impression that everything I was doing was making up for something that went wrong before. As if having a baby was the only way of repairing anything. Each small thing was correcting something else. Each minute apologizing for the one that went before. That's what I thought.

Is it possible to be saved by your own child?

It was dark by the time we got a place. Baby Maeve was asleep in a carrier basket, like it was our suitcase and we had just come in late off the ferry. We found a bed and breakfast place overlooking the harbour. I had passed it by many times before as a boy. Seaview, it was called. An ordinary name you might see repeated many times in towns all along the coast, but the name was even more familiar to me because I had said it aloud to myself so often without ever thinking that I would be one of the people going to stay there for the night. The woman running the guesthouse knew my face. She had seen me passing by many times. She was surprised to find me standing at the door so late. It must have looked like I had come back from swimming with a mother and baby and decided to stay overnight in a guest-house instead of going home. As if we had found the baby on the rocks while the tide was out. Maybe she thought I was too young, only out of school. Or maybe she thought I was only pretending to be the father. She didn't ask any questions and I didn't explain why I had no prior arrangements made. She knew where I lived. She wanted the money in advance to make sure I wouldn't change my mind halfway through the night and go home after all, leaving the baby behind.

We pretended that I was a visitor from far away, as if myself and Emily had come on holidays to the place where I had grown up. It felt so close to home without being at home. Emily was breast-feeding in the bed and I was looking out at the place where I used to go swimming, the lighthouse shining across the water towards me, the cargo ships waiting, as if we were just making it up as we went along.

28

We arrive at the restaurant a bit late. Through the
car window I can see the people inside, sitting
around the table. The white tablecloth. The faces
waiting for us. Some of them stand up when they
see her. Because she's here now, they can see the
wheelchair on the pavement. They can see her being
helped out of the car by Manfred. She has taken off
her cap, so her head is bare, that's how they recognize her now. She's looking all around, at the front
of the restaurant, at the tables outside, at the name
over the door. She wants to know where she is. What
kind of street is this and how busy is the traffic and
what else might need to be remembered? She doesn't
bother putting on her coat to go from the car into
the restaurant.

She asks Manfred would he like to join us for
lunch.

No thank you, he says. He has sandwiches made
up by his wife and he'll have them in the car.

Your little helper made your sandwiches for you,
she says.

She can be like that occasionally, Úna. She can snap from time to time, I've experienced that. The angry side in her breaks out with no warning. She can be mean, for the sake of it, not letting anyone get away with a thing.

What would you do without your little helper? she says to Manfred.

Ah, come on, Úna, I say to her. Give it up. You can't call his wife a little helper.

Manfred doesn't take offence. He must think your little helper is what you call your wife. We can't stop him calling his wife a little helper.

My little helper, he says. At the moment, my little helper is doing a doctorate in waste management. What will we do with all the baby nappies in the world? This is what she is studying, he says. So now I am her little helper for a while, Manfred says. Thank you for your kind invitation, he says, but Olga is still the best little helper for sandwiches.

Maybe Úna is disappointed that Manfred has turned down her invitation to be part of her lunch party.

I can be a bit of a bitch sometimes, she says.

Ah, you're not that bad.

A right wagon, Liam. God forgive me.

The Paris Bar is where some people say Marlene Dietrich gave her farewell party. One of her parties at least, Manfred says. Before she moved to Paris. She went to Paris to die in private and then she came back to be buried in Berlin, the round trip, Úna calls it. She's making the same round trip from Dublin to Berlin and back. Manfred has given her all the information about Marlene and he offers to drive us to the graveyard where she's buried. It's not very far, he says. It's a lovely place, a quiet city graveyard, with red-brick walls. After lunch, maybe. He has brought quite a few people there to put little stones on Marlene's grave, a train ticket, maybe, with the name of the town they come from. Only last week he tells us he brought an old man there to sit on a bench under the trees in silence.

I don't need to go to a graveyard now, she says.

Thanks, Manfred, I say on her behalf. I take the wheelchair and push her into the restaurant, then she turns to me.

Why does he want to bring me to a graveyard?

He's doing his best, Úna.

A farewell lunch. A small group of people coming to see her off at the Paris Bar. Friends and other writers she knew. A journalist. Somebody from the embassy. They've organized this lunch out of courtesy, to wish her well.

They are translating the menu for her.

Asparagus soup.

They talk as if there is nobody else at the table but her. They turn towards her and don't even see each other. She's looking into everybody's eyes, blinking a lot, smiling, nodding. She draws everyone out of themselves. Each person feels alone with her, taking turns to tell her things that will interest her.

They. Why am I saying they? We.

We are trying to cheer her up. Somebody says Berlin is a good place to radiate from. It's right in the middle of everywhere. One of the best places in

Europe to think of going to other places from. Like Poland. Warsaw. And Kraków, they say, even further east. St Petersburg. Moscow. Trans-Siberia. It's only a matter of picking where you want to go. Lots of people don't think any further. They're telling her it's a good place to get the overnight train from. And some of the trains from the east are battered by hailstones, they tell her, with white scratches along the roof, from the fierce weather. You can see the weather written on the outside of the carriages, as if it's written in Cyrillic.

She goes silent. All that talk of travelling has made her go into a dream. She loves nothing more than hearing the names, the further away the better. She says it's like Castlebar translated into Polish. Ennistymon. Milltown Malbay. Imagine Ballyvaughan in Russian. Imagine reaching Fanore in Chinese. Imagine taking the overnight train and waking up in County Clare, at Spanish Point, with the sea at your feet.

I've never been anywhere like that, she says. I've never even been to Kraków. Or St Petersburg. I'd love to go.

She tells them about travelling with Noleen. All the way down through Macedonia and Albania.

I remember a small town, she says, where a man climbed into a walnut tree for us. His feet were in the branches, shaking down the walnuts. Big green leaves like big green donkeys' ears around his head. The man said we looked like sisters and we called each other sisters, she says. Eating walnuts like sisters. I remember his wife standing by with a basket

153

in her arms and fruit flies around her head. At night we slept like sisters. I remember a cockroach running across the floor and we laughed because Noleen said it looked like he was embarrassed to be seen.

They tell her about the restaurant. They explain why it's so famous and why people wanted to be seen there before everything began to shift after the wall came down and people found new places in the east of the city to be seen in. It's a has-been restaurant, so they say, but some people still go for nostalgia. The tables are close together, the waiters are older men, wearing white aprons down to the floor. There's a cashier. Have a look at the cashier, they say. So she looks around and smiles at the cashier, a young woman wearing a white blouse sitting at a desk, high up. It's like a pulpit, she says. Not really a pulpit, more like an open-deck cubicle, a half cubicle, with a half door and the cashier sitting down, but yes, like a pulpit, too, if you like. The waiters shout numbers across the restaurant to the cashier and the cashier knows what everybody is eating.

They remember cashiers like that in Dublin. Cubicles for cashiers no longer in use. They remember all kinds of other things that have gone out of existence, like sums done on the back of brown paper bags in pencil. Things that belong to the past that you might be more likely to see if you get on the overnight train.

White asparagus, she says.

It's a big thing here in May, they tell her. White asparagus.

154

White asparagus soup.

They watch her cutting the asparagus. Her hand shakes a little as she chases a piece of it around the bowl, until she traps it with her thumb and lifts the spoon up to her mouth. And while they're talking to her, she looks around at what the others are eating, comparing what they're having to what she's having. She reaches over to take some French fries off my plate and throws them into her soup. French fries floating in the asparagus soup.

Why am I so hungry? she says.

It's great to see her eating. She's ordered lamb cutlets, and when they arrive, she picks them up and eats them by hand, holding them by the bone. She doesn't care who's looking. She's on a lot of steroids and that gives you a horse of an appetite, she says.

29

We're taking our time, sitting around the table at the Paris Bar, talking about history. About the war, going back to the Nazis. The whole twentieth century happened in Berlin, so they're saying. I wish I could remember some of the stories they were telling. But I was not fully paying attention, to be honest. Sometimes I get left behind. It's like being at school and I'm not concentrating and they have already moved on, talking about Northern Ireland when I think they're still talking about the Second World War and the Nazis. Sometimes the words used for one part of history match in with those for another part, no difference, only the names of places you have to watch out for. And the personalities. Some words, of course, you can't mistake. You know it's Ireland by the way they say let's hope so. That narrows it down. It's still in the future, at least. Or maybe only just in the recent past.

Whatever it is, they've lost me. I can't pick up the trail and I'm left thinking about irrelevant things. Personal matters that I have told her about and that have absolutely nothing to do with the people around me at the table, they wouldn't be interested.

I'm still trying to work out what was going on inside my own family. What went on after we saw my aunt and my father's brother coming out of the hotel in Cork. We had no explanation for it. We had the facts but we had no story, no context. There was a lot of talking behind closed doors. And the Jesuit, my father's brother, was no longer coming to our house with sweets in his pocket.

We were told he was on retreat. He was having a crisis in his life, that's all my mother would say. I think she wanted to tell me more but she would not allow herself. I was afraid that she might have told my brother more than me, or he was better at picking things up, and he was keeping it all to himself. She told me to pray for my father's brother because he had difficult decisions to make. He had to make up his mind whether he was still living under the same roof with the Jesuits or staying under the same roof with my aunt. We got no further explanation at the time, it was not something we were allowed to ask any more questions about.

I'm not sure my mother even had an explanation to give herself. She was left trying to figure out why my father's brother was not coming to see us any more. Had she done something wrong? I had no idea why my mother was so upset about all this. My aunt didn't come to the house any more either, on her own or with the Jesuit. We were like a family left behind. My mother kept trying to contact him but he was out of reach. She left messages, inviting him out to the house as before, she was ready to welcome him back like a real Jesuit and put him at the head of the table with a cake in the middle, his favourite coffee cake, but he wouldn't come. Maybe he was afraid of my father. Maybe he thought my father would subject him to interrogation in the front room, what was he doing coming out of a hotel in Cork arm in arm with my aunt right in front of us when he was meant to be a Jesuit?

My mother was unable to live without knowing. So one day she decided to go and see my father's brother face to face. I don't know if my father was even aware of her going to visit his brother on her own. She went on the bus, two buses in fact, to get to the red-brick house where the Jesuits lived under one roof together. She had a long walk up the drive with the windows of the building looking out over the person arriving. She said she thought she saw my father's brother watching her from one of the windows, but she didn't want to wave at him in case it was another Jesuit. She walked up the granite step and rang the bell beside the brown door. It takes a while before one of the Jesuits appears. You can hear doors opening and closing and footsteps coming along the corridor. And when a Jesuit finally comes, it's the wrong Jesuit. He let her into the reception and went to find the right Jesuit, my father's brother, our Jesuit, wherever he was, so that took more time and she was left sitting there listening out for doors opening and closing, hoping it was him, the Jesuit in our family.

She was told that my father's brother was busy,

in prayer. He could not to be disturbed. The Jesuit was very polite, as always, speaking as if he was only allowed to use the least amount of words. He said it would be a while before our Jesuit was available, so perhaps it might be better to come back another time.

My mother said she would be happy to wait.

I think it might have been an hour, maybe more. They didn't offer her anything, no tea and biscuits, only the same Jesuit coming back to see if she had gone home yet. She was sitting with her coat still on, in the small reception room, surrounded by magazines about the missions and the new schools being built. The same room where I had to meet my father's brother once or twice, for causing too much trouble at home, and once more to discuss sexual matters. Something to do with a man and a woman. That's what it was called in our family, things that happened between a man and a woman, even though it was too embarrassing to speak to my father's brother about anything at all, he didn't really have much to say about any man or any woman and neither did I, so we left it at that.

My mother said she was not leaving until she had spoken to him. And when he finally came to see her, he sat down on the far side of the room with his hands still in prayer on his knees, staring at the floor, as if she was not even in the room and it was only the holy-order magazines left.

Just tell me, my mother said.

She wanted to know the truth, that was all. She wanted to hear it from his mouth. He looked up at her and thought for a long time about what he was going to say, carefully selecting his words. But then he told her nothing, just made it clear to her that he was not going to answer any of her questions. He was even more full of silence than ever before, if that's possible, to be full of something that does not exist. He had nothing whatsoever to say to her. He was used to people confessing everything to him. He was not going to turn around and start confessing everything to my mother. She had the wrong Jesuit. What he was thinking had nothing to do with her. It was none of her business what went on between a man and a woman.

It's my business, that's all he said.

Then he got up and left her sitting there empty-handed. He didn't shake hands or embrace her. He just disappeared. She came home by the same long driveway with the well-kept lawns and the windows staring at her, two buses, the same journey in reverse with no explanation. And maybe that was the explanation.

30

There's a lot of art on the walls at the Paris Bar. Mad paintings, all the way around the entire restaurant. A light-box attached to the ceiling, illuminated in different colours with the words 'stand still and rot'. I mean, the art is pretty out there, for a restaurant. Where people are forced to eat. There is a large black-and-white photo of a man and a woman naked, in their twenties, having sex. The woman has the man's penis in her mouth. And this other couple are having their meal right next to it in silence, paying no attention whatsoever to the man in the photograph looking down with an unhappy expression on his face while the woman is leaning sideways over him with her knees apart. As if it's the most normal thing in the world for a man and a woman to have their lunch beside the man and the woman having sex, like it's all part of the same thing and you don't have to keep staring at it.

I want to know where they are now, the man and the woman in the photograph. What age are they now and do they still remember. Do they ever come back to the restaurant to look at each other? Do they maybe come back and have dinner together from time to time underneath the photo of themselves having sex? And would people know it was them having sex so close to them having dinner?

She wants to know about the artists, so they give her some of the names that are famous now. The artworks, they say, were mostly left behind by artists who were broke at the time and couldn't pay for their dinner.

I like that, she says.

Some of the art is not worth the price of a dinner.

I could leave behind a couple of words, she says.

Some of the art is worth a million dinners.

A million asparagus soups.

They tell her that a lot of famous people have come to the restaurant over the years for dinner. A lot of words have been overheard and found their way into the newspapers. A lot of words are forgotten and only the art on the walls is left when all the people who had their dinner are gone.

You can't eat art, she says.

They stand up when she stands up. That's the way I remember it. I'm narrowing down the conversations and the small talk around the edges. They talked for a while about somebody's father being her lecturer in university. There was probably a lot more said than that, but you would have to ask the others, I was not paying enough attention. I can only remember her asking herself, or asking me, why asparagus soup would make you want to cry.

I send Manfred a text giving him plenty of time

to come over, whenever he's ready. He sends me back a text to say that he is always ready. I only meant it as an expression, whenever you're ready, but he thought I meant it literally, when are you ever ready? I am here, he says. I am here always. Waiting for you and your mother, he says. Then I look out the window and see that he's been there all along, parked right outside, waiting for us.

As they're standing around and she's getting back into the wheelchair, they don't start talking to each other, ignoring her, looking to see what time it is and what they're going back to. Nobody wants to say goodbye to her. It's something they have forgotten how to do. As if there are no words for it and they cannot imagine not ever seeing her again. They wait while she's being shown around the restaurant to look at the art, without pointing at anything in particular or bothering people who might be having their dinner right next to it. The staff are smiling. Staff, I don't think she would have called them staff. The waiters are smiling and shaking her hand and saying they look forward to seeing her again.

And then I get a phone call from the Adlon, letting me know they have the tickets for *Don Carlo*. I want to tell them we don't need them. She's doing fine. I want to let them know that she's dying and she's not up to it. I'm trying to protect her from her family. I don't think it's a good idea for her to go back to see that same story again, re-enacted in front of her.

Three hundred and fifty euros each, the last tickets available.

We'll take them, she says. I'll never be here again.

So I get back to the man at the hotel reception to tell him we'll go for it. Two tickets only. So now I've booked them and we have to go.

31

I met her father once. Way back, long before I knew her. I had this job for a short while as a copy boy with the newspaper that he wrote for in Dublin. It was my duty to deliver bits of paper from one desk to another and make tea for people, get sandwiches and biscuits and buttered rock buns, sometimes a burger, sometimes a kebab. The journalists were always using their pens to stir the tea and leaving the teabags on the table, staining an old newspaper.

Her father was rarely seen in his office, only occasionally when he came back late in the evening to write his column. He was standing at the top of the stairs one day on his way out, that's how I remember it, just as I was going up. I had no dealings with him. I didn't talk to him. I didn't shake his hand. I'm not in a position to say what he was like as a father. I can't even say that I met him, properly, only that he stood in front of me and smiled as if he wanted to talk to me. I remember him wearing a carnation in his lapel, like he was coming from a wedding. Or maybe he just made Dublin look like there was always somebody getting married.

He was in no hurry. He looked me in the eyes and I felt he knew me for some reason, but it was only that I knew him. He was checking to see if I was somebody. Anybody. He gave me a chance to say who I was and where I was from and who my mother and father were and what school I went to, if I was related to anyone in public life. He waited to see if I had anything to reveal, that is, if I knew anything interesting about anyone at all that was worth remembering, anything worth passing on or publishing in a newspaper column. He said good evening to me, but I forgot how to speak. I didn't have the words put together in the right order in my head. I couldn't get the sentence I was hoping to say off the ground. I wanted to tell him everything I knew, but I didn't know what that was yet.

To my mind, he looked OK. I liked him. My first impression was all I had to go by and that gave me no reason to believe otherwise. He seemed like a good enough father from the outside. He had silver hair and his eyes were clear. His chest was out. His shoulders were square. He wore a light-coloured suit, his shoes were polished and he looked very solid, like he never needed help from anyone, like he never missed a bus or got caught in the rain, like he never found the shops closed and nowhere to get milk, all those ordinary things that people had to think about seemed to be far from his mind. He looked trouble-free. Like he never lost his temper and he never had a bad word to say about anyone, somebody who was liked by everyone, with no guilt and nothing to answer for. He looked welcoming, like he shook hands with people a lot, like he remembered everybody's name.

He gave me the impression that he wanted to have a conversation with me and I could come back to him once I had something to remember. He took his time passing me by and I turned around at the top of the stairs. He stopped at the bottom of the stairs for a moment to check the carnation in his jacket. And by the time I got the words right in my head he was already gone.

I said good evening to the smile that was left behind.

When I read her book years later, I could not believe this was the same man I had seen passing me on the stairs. His smile made me think that he had a lovely family and I could only imagine that if I had had a father like that myself, my problems would be over. He seemed full of calmness. Like he had no anger in him. Like he owned a yacht or an American car or maybe that he knew how to fly a plane. Maybe he could have been an actor in a movie at some point, or that he was good with cards and knew lots of tricks and stories that he could entertain people with.

I didn't want to believe that he murdered his own son.

She said her father was just like the King in *Don Carlo* and he killed her brother.

Not that I'm arguing with her memory, but I still

think of her father well. I thought she was exaggerating. And you know something, I never told her that I met him. I didn't want to bring it up. I didn't have the heart to tell her that he didn't look as bad as he was.

What am I saying? This is what I'm saying. At the end of her first book she said she could forgive her parents. And then, at the end of the second book she says her parents are murderers and she could never forgive them. So I was only thinking it would not be all that difficult to persuade her to go back to the first version again, that's all.

I think forgiveness is a bit overrated. They keep going on about it nowadays. Open up. Forgive the past. Especially things you can do nothing about. Things you cannot possibly change at this point, like where you entered your life. You have to forgive yourself, that's what they say. They have a new way of speaking about all these things, like they never raise their voices and nobody ever loses their temper any more in Ireland. You hear them on the radio now with that suave voice, the new spiritual, she calls it.

She was not letting anybody off the hook, especially now.

Nothing will ever change if you go all soft, Liam. You can't look back all soggy with nostalgia, she said, everything is all right, nobody meant any harm, sure let's all forget about it and be nice and enjoy our lives. She could not take the dishonesty of it, like people going back to Mass, people saying they miss the way things were under Communism.

I'm not changing my story, she said.

It must have been around the same time, when I saw her father on the stairs, that she came back from London to live in Dublin again. It could have been the same evening for all I know. Her father found out where she was living and went to see her, just turned up at the door. She had come back to Ireland to say all the things that were unsaid. All the things that Irish people didn't know how to say about themselves yet, so many things that needed to be confronted out loud. Everything inside the family had always been kept inside the family, that was the rule up to that time, with no outside interference. It was none of anyone's business outside the front door, only the priest and God. Things were bad enough economically without bringing private, social matters out into the open, and she came back to Dublin to take the roof off the family. She was walking straight into all the houses in Ireland that were still keeping their secrets.

Her father was furious with her. He heard what people were saying around the city. He was furious at her curly hair and the freedom of speech she was allowing herself. He didn't think a woman could be so much like him, least of all his own daughter, drinking like her mother and sleeping around like her father. Maybe he was afraid of her revealing things about him, killing his own son. That whole *Don Carlo* thing going on inside the family.

It wasn't time yet for the rhythm of honesty.

Her father was standing in her flat, she said. It was nothing more than a bedroom with a kitchen in it. All she could do was smile at him, because she was paying her own rent and her own electricity bills and that made him even more furious, her independence. She was not a helpless woman. All he could do was shout. And she kept smiling. He said she would be nobody without him, if he hadn't sold his car and borrowed another car to get her into boarding school and save her from married men. What made him most angry was that she was pretending not to be his daughter any more, even though everyone knew who she was. No matter how famous he was, he had no power over her any longer. He threatened her. She never felt so much alone with a man before as with her own father. And the only way that he could think of losing his temper was to kick something. He kicked the cupboard underneath the sink. The door of the cupboard opened with the force of it. The bin fell out, spilling the contents across the room. They both stared at what he had done and she wrote it all down in her memory, her collection. He walked out and left the tea leaves scattered on the floor behind him.

32

They've installed a hydraulic lift out in the open, outside the Pergamon Museum. Getting Úna up the steps would have been impossible, even for myself and Manfred together. Manfred wheels her onto the ramp and secures the wheelchair to make it safe, then closes the gate. She's smiling like a child, she loves it. As if she's at a funfair, going up slowly with the magnificent building behind her, all those large windows, the canal around the front and the overhead trains going by in the distance.

The Pergamon Altar is great. I know the Nazis loved it, she says, let's not forget that. But that doesn't stop you admiring the sheer size of it, like a city inside a huge room. It makes you feel small and powerless. The altar with the wide marble steps and the temple at the top is only a tiny fragment of the city, you can check that on the scale model. And around the walls are these marble carvings showing what people were up to in those days.

Figures of semi-naked men and women. Some peaceful scenes, women bathing, children playing, men carrying fruit. And war. Plenty of war. Arms and legs missing, never found or reattached by archaeologists. Horses with missing heads. Chariots. People in rage. People in agony. A lion biting into the leg of a man, all that kind of thing.

There was an echo around the hall, I remember. Groups of people with blue earphones on, listening to the history being replayed as they walked around. People sitting on the marble steps talking, calling each other. And children. A small girl shouting, testing the echo. I could not find out where the child's voice was actually coming from. I checked all the children there, so in the end, I thought it might have been a child in one of the sculptures. From the past. A child of Pergamon still echoing around the room.

I went up the steps to the top of the altar and waved down at her from the temple. She smiled back at me. And maybe it was all that marble around us that made me think of her as part of the story of ancient Greece. Seeing her from a distance, sitting there waving at me, gave me the feeling that I was looking back over her life, like one of those archaeologists. All these questions I had not even thought of asking yet.

There were things I couldn't let go. As a father myself. I felt I had to speak up for her father, out of his mouth. I got back down and pushed the wheel-chair into the next room. It was quieter in there with lots of stone columns and assorted bits of anatomy in no human order, arms and heads and half men, like a puzzle waiting to be put back together. I found

172

a place behind a pillar and decided to ask her what exactly happened to her brother. I wanted to know the truth, because I couldn't imagine being murdered by my own father.

Úna, I said to her. Did your father really kill your brother?

Yes. He was murdered.

How?

They gave him his life.

Come on, Úna. That's not murder.

My brother had a terrible life, she said.

That's a serious accusation. Murder. I know people use the word all the time in a light-hearted way. But still and all, I said, calling your own father a murderer.

She looked astonished. She could not believe I would turn on her like this, in the Pergamon Museum of all places.

Listen, Liam. My father killed my brother when he sent him to London with no love in him.

Premeditated.

Liam. My brother had a hole in his chest where love went right through him. He had no protection, Liam, no defence. He had no way of forming a normal relationship with the world. You see him in a photograph before he went away and he looks great, very handsome, like he had everything going for him. Then you see him in another photograph some years later and he's a wreck, like he's lived a hundred lives. He never learned how to respect himself or find anyone else to respect him. Something destroyed him early on, in his childhood. I'm not going into all this here, Liam, but his father might as well have taken his life at birth because he sent him off with nothing. Nothing. Nothing. I swear to God, Liam.

I would hate my daughter calling me a murderer.

Don't compare yourself to my father, she said.

I'm only saying, Úna. Your father was human, not somebody in an opera.

What?

Well, that was it. I thought she was trying to stand up out of the wheelchair and walk away. She shouted my name across the room so that everyone in that part of the museum suddenly turned to look at us.

Liam, she shouted. You have no right to question me. My father took my brother from me. I'm not going to forgive him for that, as long as I live.

The visitors at the museum were beginning to pay more attention to us than to the ancient artefacts. They were probably wondering what I had done to her. She was helpless, sitting in a wheelchair with her head bare from radiation, unable to escape from my questions.

My brother was too afraid, she said, too alone, too damaged to live a normal life. What do you call that, Liam? That's murder. My mother and father took everything that belonged to us. They gave us our lives and they stole them back again. My father not only stole my brother, she said, he stole my children from me too. The children I could never have, Liam, because I was afraid they might end up like my brother. I was afraid of what I saw in his eyes. I was

174

afraid of what my brother had seen happening when he was a child, what he could never talk about.

She was holding on to her anger.

Yes, she said. I am holding on to my anger. Because that's all I have left. My family, my anger, my grudge. My family rage, whatever you want to call it, Liam. What you get from your father and mother. From your country. What you spend the rest of your life trying to escape from. Things that follow you. It's what made me want to get even with the world, in my own words. It's the artistic rage, Liam. Every writer has that rage, she said, otherwise they wouldn't be writers, they'd be too special, too much apart from the rest of us. Without that rage they'd be too obsessed with genius, they'd sound just like priests, or cardinals, making a holy cult of themselves. They wouldn't be good writers, they wouldn't be human enough without their own little line of anger and guilt and grudge and envy and failure and desperately wanting to be loved more than anyone else in the world.

Don't take that away from me, Liam.

I had to let it go. It felt too much like the final judgement, interrogating her about her father in a place like this. I turned the wheelchair around and pushed her towards the exit. It looked as though she was being removed like a noisy child.

I forgive nobody, she said.

It's all right, Úna.

I wish them all the fires and ice of hell.

Calm down.

Beckett was right, she said. If only I had thought

175

up those words myself. I wish them all an atrocious life. I wish them lots of delays, cancellations, no refunds. I hope there's always somebody ahead of them in the queue. And in the life hereafter, she said, they can have an honoured name as far as I'm concerned.

Don't start going like Beckett, I said.

Look what they did to him, she said. They named a bridge after him.

The Beckett Bridge.

It's unforgivable.

That's a beautiful bridge, I said.

It's an atrocity, she said. A bridge over the river Liffey. He would freak out if he heard that. I'm serious, if he was still alive today, the poor man, he would put an end to it, right now, he would go no further. Not for another second. They waited until he was dead so he could not object to it himself, in person.

It's like a musical instrument, I said.

Exactly, she said. A bridge in the shape of a harp. For Samuel Beckett, of all people. Think about it, Liam. A fucking bridge over the Liffey in the shape of an Irish harp.

Calm down, you're in Berlin.

I got her as far as the souvenirs and told her to keep her voice down. I told her I'd make sure there would be no bridges named after her.

She was laughing again.

What would you say to a roundabout? I asked her.

I swear to God, Liam.

I leaned down behind her and whispered in her ear. There might be one or two roundabouts in Limerick still unnamed, I told her. Every time people come to the roundabout they'll think of you, I said, wouldn't that be nice? Then she half-turned around in the wheelchair and said she would come back and kill me. She would kill the whole lot of us.

33

I've got her a small brochure about the history of the Pergamon Altar. I've bought her a drink of apple juice mixed with fizzy water, a cloudy drink. I ask her would she like a cake and she wants a scone. Do they not have any fruit scones and jam, raspberry jam? Blackberry jam, I don't suppose they have that, she says. They have no scones in the café at the Pergamon Museum, so I get her one of those almond cakes, like a horseshoe with both ends dipped in chocolate. She loves those. She's eaten hers very quickly so I give her one of the remaining chocolate ends off my horseshoe as well. She drinks the apple juice and takes some more pills and I ask her is everything all right now?

I'm fine, she says.

She starts taking things out from her see-through bag. She places them on the table one by one, her medication, her reading glasses, the room key, the nail clippers, the mobile phone, switched off. All the contents out on the table for everyone to see. As if she was at home. She looks at each item individually.

She examines the tub of hand cream as though she's never seen it before, reading the label, holding it away from her to look at the design on the lid, seeing what's underneath, reading the label a second time, opening it up to smell it and closing the lid again. Then she picks a spot on the table for it. She looks into her bag once more, outside and inside. She takes out more and more things, I don't know what for, does she want to make sure she's got everything?

Liam, she says. We better not forget the sheets.

No problem, I'll remind Manfred.

She has an overview. She's playing dominoes with her things, shifting them around on the table to make the display more logical, creams together, hotel belongings together, reading materials with reading materials. She looks at everything in front of her on the table, all in order.

I'm only putting this together now.

She's thinking back, wondering what more she could have done for her brother. She talks about him coming to see her on her birthday once. He was living up in the north of London at that stage, Wood Green, I think she said it was. She's talking about how she hardly ever got to see him. And one day she found him standing in the reception, where she was working. He was talking to the porter at the door. Her brother was the image of his father, she says, chatting to the nearest person available to see what story they had. He had come to bring me out for a drink on my birthday, she says. Even though he didn't really have the money to stand a drink. And I had already arranged to go out with friends, colleagues from work. So I was caught between the two. He was standing there with a big smile on his face and I had to introduce him to everyone, she says, what else could I do? I brought him with me to the pub and they all loved him. They were buying him drink and he was really happy, telling stories.

For a moment, she says, I thought it was great having a brother, like some kind of credentials, so people knew I came from a normal family where everyone drank and sang songs around the table. But I knew where this was headed, she says. I could see the thin façade I had going for myself in London was steadily being dismantled. There was no telling what he would say. I was about to be found out. Having my brother around was like wearing my heart on my sleeve, she says.

At one point, she got her brother up to the bar so he could help carry a round of drinks back to the table. It was the only way she could talk to him privately.

Don't start getting any ideas, she said to him, you're not here for the night.

He kept getting more and more drunk, she says, just like his own mother. It was the only thing he ever learned at home, how to look forward to the next drink, how to go all the way and get properly out of the head. I didn't know what to do with him, she says. You know the way it is, you can dismiss your own brother and think of him as a failure, until you're in company and you feel you have to be nice to him, in front of people. You see other people taking him seriously. You see what they see in him, the pity they have for him. It was the disaster in my brother that reminded me of the potential disaster in myself, she says. I was afraid they could see that whole family disaster coming out bit by bit the more drunk he got.

So I got him out of there, she says. When the next opportunity arose, she says, I took him by the arm like we were the best family in the world. I made excuses, she says. I told them we had to go because we were expecting a call from home. Which was a big lie. There was nothing I wanted more than to keep drinking with my brother and my friends, if they even were friends, but I had to stop him before he got totally paralysed and let me down. I didn't want him to see me being myself either. So I sent him off in a taxi, God forgive me, she says, all the way up to Wood Green, it cost me a fortune. Imagine that, Liam, I packed my brother off in a taxi to whatever Godforsaken place he was living and I went back to the even sadder, Godforsaken place where I was living, just to be on my own, on my birthday.

I didn't know how to help him, she says. I didn't think it was up to me. I was his big sister but I had no idea. I should have given him things to do. Some kind of task to carry out. Something to get him started. Something he could be proud of.

Then she turns to me and wants to know would I do her a favour. After she's gone, that is, would I go somewhere she's never been before.

Where?

If I had children, she says, that's what I would

do. I would give them tasks to carry out. I would send them all over the world, places I could never get to. Go to Tibet, that sort of thing. Go to one of their temples. Bring me back something, I would say to them, she says. Come back with a stick or a small piece of cloth. Dried fruit. Anything at all.

Will you do me a favour, Liam? After me. Will you go to Kraków? I always wanted to go to Kraków. Please, Liam, will you do that for me?

34

I told her what it was like being a father. I told her that once you become a parent yourself you keep wondering if there's something you have deprived your child of and you hope it's not love.

I told her about my daughter, when she was only four years of age. She went ahead of me one day, at top speed, on her scooter. She went down the hill, waving at the rabbits in the window of the pet shop, all the way down past the church. No sense of danger. I was shouting after her to stop but she kept going. She was miles ahead and I was sure she would end up going straight on to the main road. I ran after her. I legged it as fast as I could, with all these Italian students across the road laughing at me. And at the bottom of the road she disappeared around the corner and fell off. I picked her up and held her in my arms and I felt so lucky that she was all right, unharmed.

What are you saying, Liam?

I couldn't stop my daughter growing up and asking questions, I said. Maeve. She must have overheard. Because she was upstairs when I was asking Emily all these questions I should never have asked. It was my last chance not to ask questions. But that's the truth for you, it's like a hair in your mouth. Emily was standing in the kitchen saying she was not going to answer any questions, why should she? It was not a question she was able to answer. And I kept saying I didn't believe her. My question was following her around the house, out on to the patio while she suddenly had to look after some potted plants in semi-darkness, back into the house the question was still following her into the bathroom while she was going to the loo and she asked me to let her close the door at least, through the hallway while she was putting on her coat, searching for something in her bag as though the answer was there all along. And Maeve was standing at the window upstairs watching while Emily was walking out the front door not knowing where to go from there, stopping to look right and left on the pavement, and me still asking her to come back and answer the question.

What question?

Like, am I the real father?

Is there some doubt?

It finally came out because of the wedding, I explain. Everything is up in the air because the wedding is not happening, it's been cancelled. All these second thoughts that Maeve is having. She feels it's better not to commit to anything, as if she's only going to be repeating all the mistakes that went before her, as if there's something keeping her from starting her life.

It was me who gave her that doubt, I point out. All these second thoughts she picked up from me in the first place. Doubts I should have been keeping to myself and which were suddenly out in the open.

One evening she came out to see me on her own. Just Maeve and myself, the two of us alone in the house. I had everything ready, laid out on the table. She came in and kissed me. Then she passed me by and dropped her bag in the middle of the hallway, by the stairs. She threw her coat on the sofa and looked around as usual and said, Jesus, look at the place, Dad. You're so fucking tidy, it's unbelievable. Because she was always accusing me of tidying around people, saying there was nothing I enjoyed more in life than clearing up, coming to the end of a packet, or a carton, a bottle of shampoo, getting the dishwasher stacked properly. She said I behaved as if I wanted to be invisible, as if I didn't want to leave any evidence behind. As if real people were too real for me and I could not bear them leaving their belongings around the place. At least give me a chance to make a mess, Dad, before you start picking things up. She said you had to leave some trace of yourself behind or else you don't exist. So I left her bag where it was in the hallway and her coat on the sofa, with one arm reaching down towards the floor. I was glad to see them there, where they were dropped.

I asked Maeve did she want something to eat but she didn't, not even cake. I told her the silver stud in her bottom lip looked great, but that's not what she came to hear.

When she came into the kitchen it felt as though we were going to have dinner together. Maeve sat at one end of the table and I sat at the other. It was no big deal, just a formality. We read through the instructions first and there was no need to say too much or keep looking at each other. I think we both wanted to get on with it. It was a bit embarrassing, to be honest, so unnecessary. So we just moved on as if it was no more than a form to be filled in together. Tax returns or something like that. I licked my swab. She licked her swab at the other end of the table. We had to keep things very separate, that was important to bear in mind. Because you can't allow the colours to get mixed up. Otherwise everybody is related to one another and there is no way of proving anyone apart. So we did all that. As per the instructions. I had the green envelope and she had the pink one. There was a third blue envelope which would have been for the mother, but there was no dispute over her and no need for that extra one, Emily was not present. Then Maeve and myself put the two envelopes, the green one and the pink one, into the big envelope and we threw the other one out, the blue one. And that's where we stood, so to speak, in doubt, unresolved.

It felt like being on one of those reality shows,

Jerry Springer, there must be a million stories like it all over the world, I thought. This must be going on in every town in Ireland, Europe, anywhere. It felt like we were in one of those TV dramas, maybe inside an opera, even older than that, something that's been going on in families for centuries, since the beginning of time. There was no sense in getting emotional about it, saying things that could not be revoked. I think we tried to behave quite normally, as though nothing was happening. We carried on as always, like father and daughter, not taking too much notice of each other.

Although.

There was one moment where Maeve and I made eye contact, I remember. Across the table, we looked at each other as if we were both saying what? What are we doing here? Only we didn't say anything at all. It was nothing more than a brief look, directly in the eyes. It was filled with a million passing questions, going back and forth in a great hurry. Like how come we were sitting here in the same room together? We could be people who never met before, we could have been in different lives coming from different families and never laid eyes on each other until now. It was so ridiculous, we smiled. A quick smile, just to confirm how close we were and how many things we could remember together, so much stuff that didn't even need to be said. But we were also examining each other, checking each other out, as they say. Because everything was up for comparison. Everything that was familiar was being questioned, like going through the family check-list, everyone does it. Ticking off. Measuring. Eyes, nose, cheekbones. The laugh, the voice, the whole person you are, the kind of jokes you make.

All those thoughts were listed off in that smile, nothing hidden. It was a moment of honesty. We were sharing something, I suppose you could say. Sharing, that's a terrible word, completely misappropriated. Why is your child not sharing? We're disappointed that your child has not learned to share yet like the other children, they said when Maeve was in Montessori. Today we are going to learn how to share, OK? I don't know about those words they impose on children. It's like the word connection, or the word included. They can be so meaningless, so unhelpful, so common to everyone and nobody. Maybe it was more of a confirmation, if you can even trust that word. Because there was something in that smile between myself and my daughter that made us both feel so included, so connected, so much like a confirmation, like we were sharing something that involved nobody else in the world, nobody else could have come to claim any part in it, we were in the same place, in the same life, in the same stretch of time together.

It felt like an attempt at clearing up our family story, like tidying up the house, turning it into a show house, no trace of anyone actually living there, ready to rent. That's what my life suddenly looked like to me. Unoccupied. I was smiling at her, trying to make sure she understood that she was still part of the same family disorder, I suppose, that not everything was tidy, we were leaving a trace.

I wanted to say something along those lines to Maeve, something father to daughter. I mentioned the wedding, which was a mistake. I was encouraging her to go ahead with it, asking her what kind of music she was thinking of having, a DJ or a band? I suppose I was looking for practical things to say, not realizing that the less I said about the wedding the better.

Maeve looked at her phone.

I asked her did she want to stay and have a drink, would we open a bottle of wine? She raised her head up from her phone as if she was blinded by the sun. What? Again it was the silent word, what? Was this the right moment for a drink? Had I suddenly discovered something to celebrate in all this? She got up from the table and said it was time for her to go. She went around picking up everything she had brought with her, one by one in reverse order, her phone, her coat, her bag, making sure to leave nothing behind. Then we walked out the front door and went to the nearest postbox down on the main street. We posted the envelope together, you know, in each other's presence, because that's what you're meant to do, to make sure nobody has tampered with the evidence in the meantime.

I put my arms around Maeve, and, of course, she returned the embrace. I knew it was important not to make it look like we were saying goodbye. She was not going away anywhere, she was not leaving, only going home, back to her place. And she didn't want me standing in the street watching her walking away as if she would never be seen again, the way

189

I used to do when she was going to school. Waiting for her when she came out of school again as if I hadn't moved from the spot. I knew not to do that. Be cool about this, she said to me. Only she didn't say that. I just heard myself saying it for her.

35

I spoke to Maeve on the phone as soon as the result came back and she was not saying very much, neither of us were. We're not related, Maeve and me. She still kept calling me Dad. I suppose it takes time to get out of the habit of saying that. Dad, she said, are you still there? Dad? Because I was silent, as if I had turned off the phone. I had no idea what to say to her. It was all a bit of a transition for me. I felt myself sweeping back over everything as if my life had been a mistake. My memory was not to be trusted. It was all being questioned. It felt like having nothing to hold on to, nothing to go by.

You never suspected? Úna asked me.

Well, yes, I kind of knew. You know and you don't know, at the same time. I didn't want to know, I suppose. And now that I know, I'm trying to tell myself it doesn't matter. Who cares who the father is, I'm fine with all that. It has no substance, it's only proof. I don't have to believe the proof. It was knowing and not knowing, that was the problem. I wanted to be the owner of my life with my daughter in it. I should never have started following Emily with questions she could not answer. I was trying to find out something I should not have been hoping to find out, that's all.

You're still her father, Liam. She's still your daughter.

No question, I said.

Of course she's my daughter. I brought her up. It was me who brought her out to Tallaght Hospital when she was only four to get a blood test, just a precaution really, we thought she was too small for her age. I was afraid she might have stopped growing. I remember telling Maeve this long story to keep her distracted while the nurse was getting the needle ready, all about a stormy night with lots of big words like ferocious winds and mountainous waves. It was me who made sure nothing was wrong with her, only that she was not very tall, and her height was always something she could compensate for, she'll look great in a pair of high heels, so the consultant said at the time. It was me who helped her with her homework, I explained how fermenta-tion works, the solar system. I made her sandwiches for school, that sort of thing. All the journeys we went on together, the large stones we brought back from Kerry with us in the car, I know that's not very ecological now. Big oval stones, glossy in the rain. The eggs of a dinosaur, so we believed and maybe she still believes that, I hope so. All the photographs I have of her sitting on the stones. All the stories we made up about dinosaurs hatching and how we had to bring them back to the beach in Ventry where they came from, because that's where the dinosaurs live.

This is the proof that I am her father, as far as I'm concerned. The stories. The photographs. The school reports. All those times she came back from being away on holiday with her mother, visiting Emily's parents in Canada, how much she had grown in three weeks, all the things I had to catch up with, the whole trip, from what the flight attendant said to her to what she saw along the straight roads of Ontario, the cornfields like forests where they said children sometimes get lost and are not found again until the corn is harvested.

I've kept all the things that made her afraid and all the things that made her laugh. I still have the drawing she made of a castle with three entrances, one where you climb up a ladder, another one where you climb up by this long plait of hair, and also across a bridge straight through the main door. I have everything. I've even kept her mispronunci-ations, the family words, I suppose you call them, like what in earth, instead of what on earth. Like coldy and warmy, instead of cold and warm.

That's the only proof, I swear.

What else is there to be said? Apart from the fact that this was my story, the story I told to Úna in Berlin, that's who I am now. I am the story of doubt and never being sure and always having to prove that I am the only father that matters. I am the story of a man who loves his daughter even more because of all this doubt, the story of a man who would not exist without the story of his daughter.

So yes, absolutely I'm still her father, one hundred percent, just not biologically.

Ah Liam, Úna says.

She begins to take all her things off the table, throwing them back into the see-through bag in no particular order. As if they don't matter very much now and all the care she took in placing them on the table was for nothing. All on top of each other, including the Pergamon brochure. The medication was the last to go in and she rattled the Xanax in the air, offering me more. What harm? I take another one, just to be myself again.

36

Manfred is bringing her back down in the hydraulic lift. She's waving at me and holding her see-through bag against her chest with the other arm. He helps her out of the lift and straight into the wheelchair, which he's already left at the bottom of the steps. The car is waiting with the sliding door open, but instead of getting back in, she decides to go for a walk. She wants to see a bit of the area, on foot, so to speak. She takes my hand and gets Manfred to push the wheelchair. We walk side by side, not saying anything, just holding hands. We walk around the island of museums, past other museums we could have gone into if only we had more time. We stop for a while on a bridge. It's still warm enough out and she has her cap on. I want to take a photograph, but she tells Manfred to take it instead, with myself and Úna together.

She won't let go of my hand in the photograph either. We're like a couple. She's smiling and I'm smiling.

I think she's trying to distract me from myself, so

she starts asking Manfred questions. Where did they get married? How did he meet his wife? And what time of the year did they get married? Manfred answers all the questions in reverse order. He says he got married in May, around this time of the year. He met Olga at a cookery course. They got married here in Berlin. It was a funny time for us, Manfred says, a big wedding with a great mixture of people from Turkey and Poland and Germany.

He says the Turkish side of the family were the noisiest. You cannot imagine, he says. His cousins got the entire fleet of cars out for the day, everybody blazing their horns, he says. Blazing, is this correct?

Blaring, she says.

Yes, blaring, he says. Blaring. Blaring. We do this in Berlin, like in Turkey. We drive through the streets to let everybody know that somebody is getting married.

I know what you're saying, she says. It puts people in a great mood. You want to catch a glimpse of the bride's face passing by.

Manfred tells us that his cousins stopped the whole fleet of cars on Potsdamer Platz. Crazy, he says. In the middle of the junction. Many beautiful cars, Mercedes, Lexus, BMW, mostly black, he says, decorated with ribbons. And Turkish flags. Like Potsdamer Platz was deep in Turkey, a village in Antalya, can you imagine? The men and women got out and danced, he says. Me and Olga had to get out and join them, in the street. The traffic was held up for five minutes, more. Very crazy.

Manfred shows us some pictures on his phone.

And the police didn't interfere, Úna says.

By the time the police come, he says, everyone is gone. I am a driver myself, he says. I have seen it many times. You see a wedding and you say, OK, relax, this will take time. If you are in a hurry, please take a different route.

We look at the pictures of Manfred and his bride Olga dancing in the street with the Sony Centre in the background. The car doors are left open behind them. Ribbons and brightly coloured scarves tied to the wing mirrors. The wedding guests dancing in a circle, holding hands. A dancing human chain, if you like. Women in long dresses. Big men linking up with their little fingers, so it seems to me.

Can you imagine, Manfred says. On Potsdamer Platz. Blazing horns everywhere, very crazy. It was so funny for us, he says. Dancing with the music from the car. People were standing on the street watching. Very crazy. Very crazy. The men were whistling, he says. And some of the women were screaming. No. Shouting. Down at the back of the throat.

Ululating, she says.

Yes, Manfred says. The women were doing that and the men were whistling. Then everyone got back into their cars. My cousins directed the traffic and we were all gone again.

You could pick up a few ideas, Liam, she says.

I come through Potsdamer Platz twenty times a day, Manfred says, and every time I want to blaze the horn, just to remember.

You should, she says. Manfred, absolutely, you

should do it for Olga, no matter who you have in the car. Will you promise? You must do that.

Very crazy, he says.

Then we're back in the car again and Manfred has forgotten to switch off the radio. He's left the station on and we can hear the voice a woman singing. Úna asks him what the music is. Is it Turkish music? Yes, he says. It's more Berlin-Turkish music, like hip-hop Turkish, you might say.

I love this, she says. Turn it up, Manfred.

She opens her window and lets the music off the lead, out into the streets, full blast. The singer's voice sounds very young, twisting in all directions. Of course we have no idea what the words are, so we can imagine anything we like. She might be singing about love, like most pop songs, I suppose, maybe she's singing about a wedding. Out in the open, with the sun going down. And her head shaking from side to side. Like she's bending over backwards until her hair is touching the ground.

37

Holding hands. It was not like her to hold hands, they told me after the funeral. Man or woman. She was not the type of person you could put your arm around without warning, they said, she didn't like you hanging out of her like a schoolgirl. Something in her childhood made her afraid of affection. Even in the company of those who loved her.

Noleen loved her, so they told me. They said Noleen loved her and she wanted to see the photographs of Berlin, so I passed them on.

They told me about the time in Dublin when there was a big group of them sitting around the table in a restaurant. Journalists and writers, people from the TV. Everybody was arguing about what was happening at the time in Northern Ireland, then they turned around to see Noleen with her arm around Úna. So that became the news instead, women in Dublin falling in love with each other.

We were looking over the photographs of her in Berlin and they said it was not like her to wear a baseball cap either. She normally left her curls out for the rain. I told them it was my baseball cap to keep her warm.

They told me that when she was travelling with Noleen in Romania, she once gave away all her money to a woman in the street. It was an enormous amount of money, apparently, so they said, too much and not enough. The woman looked at the money in her hand as if it was poison. She hid the money in the top of her dress, they said, then she picked up her child and fled. But then Úna and Noleen were worried what her husband would think, would he be asking her if she had turned herself into a prostitute with the child for that kind of money, so they went looking for her, not to take the money back, only to explain to her husband that they had given it to her in good faith.

I told them that she told me that story in Berlin.

They said she came from a time of big families. When there was not much money around. When there was plenty of alcoholism. When there was always some child sick with breathing trouble. A time when you were told to put your head over a basin of hot water and eucalyptus oil, breathing in and out, hold it, hold it, as long as possible, with a towel over your head like a hood. That was the solution to all breathing problems. The basin on one chair and you sitting on another chair underneath a tent, with all that steam. And you were to stay in there until you were suffocating and it was sheer relief to come up for air again and breathe normally. In kitchens all over the country there were heads under towels, they said.

They told me how she got drunk one night at a party in Dublin and drove straight out to the west, down to Clare, in the middle of the night. It was close to Christmas, they said, and even with all the people around her at the party she felt alone. And after all that drinking she went home and got the dog, Buddy, and the cat she had that time, then she drove through the night with all the towns going backwards past her and all the Christmas lights on in the houses, until she got as far as Clare, speeding along the narrow winding roads and she ended up crashing the car, turned over, so they said. That's the way she was found, upside down in the ditch, they said, lucky to be alive. Not even injured, they said. She was more worried about the cat gone missing. Buddy stayed with her but the cat was gone, so the next day she put an appeal out on the radio to say that she would be spending Christmas alone and her cat was missing somewhere along the road around Corafin, or was it Ennistymon they said? She said herself and Buddy would be so lonely and worried, looking out the window at the rain, but then the guards arrived at the door of her cottage two days later with the cat.

They told me that she never wanted to be perfect. She loved mistakes. She loved people who allowed their mistakes to be seen. She loved all the accidental things that people said and did quite innocently without thinking too much beforehand, things that were said and done without people trying them out in their heads beforehand. They remembered her saying that some people used words like make-up and some people used words like food and some people used words like sunglasses, to avoid people looking into their eyes. They said she could be mean at times, or impatient, or thoughtless, maybe that was the word they used. Obsessed with herself. They told me how she was once invited to give a talk at an event in Galway with a poet. The venue was packed out as always, the poet never had such a big audience before. But then she insisted on going first and she talked for almost two hours, answering questions at length. There was no time for the poet, they said, because when she was finished talking, people came rushing up to get their books signed. Then she left and the audience left with her.

There was nothing I could think of adding to that. I was not there to defend her. All I said was that she was very generous to the waitress.

I told them she didn't like to be confined. She had to have the hotel-room window open at night. She didn't like being inside in the conservatories, at the Botanic Garden, because it was too hot and she couldn't breathe.

They told me how she loved being alone with the light coming in from the street. She loved the head-lights of cars going backwards across the ceiling in her house in Dublin. They remembered her saying how she loved the voices of drunken people outside the window, all the fights going by and the sound of bottles and cans and pissing and puking and laughing and women screeching in their bare feet because their high heels were killing them, women shouting fuck and bitch and cunt, you fucking bitch, they said, and the songs people sometimes burst into at night with no intention of finishing, only the first two lines before they were gone out of reach again.

I told them that she got lost in the hotel in Berlin.

How could she get lost in a hotel? The Adlon of all places?

I explained that I had to go and talk to Manfred. Manfred the driver, I said, to make sure that was clear. All we had left to do at that point was get to *Don Carlo*, the opera. The State Opera was within walking distance, there was no need for the car. It was up to me to go and tell Manfred while she went up to her room to be alone for a while. I brought her as far as the elevator. I thought she would be fine from there. She was well able to manage. She had the room key in her hand.

You let her go, they said.

She wanted to manage, I said.

I told them that I took care of her see-through bag, just to make it easier for her. I should have stayed with her, I know, but she waved her hand and told me to go back out and talk to Manfred. You see Manfred was insisting on waiting for us after the opera, just in case it started raining. He kept saying that he didn't want me and my mother walking back in the rain. She was not my mother, of course, but I didn't want to disown her. And he said it was not a question of extra money for him or anything like that, just a favour he would like to do for us. I will be outside the opera house, Manfred said. But she would not hear of it. You will not be outside the opera house, she had said to Manfred already. There was not going to be any raining. I had to go and make sure he understood that he was to go home to Olga and the children, right now, and stay there. He was not to come out again and he was not to be at the opera house.

They could not believe I brought her to see *Don Carlo*.

It was her last chance.

Don Carlo?

She really wanted to go, I said.

They explained to me how her brother came back from London. He was pretty bad at that point when she got him home to Dublin. If home is still a good word for home, in his case, they said. Home is the only word you have for what you remember, they said, what's left behind, what her brother was trying to get back to, what he kept inside all this time. He had nothing going for him, so they told me. He had the years of an older man inside the face of a young man. He was very thin. His teeth were bad. His mother and father were both dead at this stage. He still had the eyes of his father, but his memory was gone with all the people walking in and out of his life, helping themselves. He looked as though nothing meant anything to him, and coming home was even harder than going away. There was nobody enquiring for him, nobody around who really knew him. The city had moved on without him. The streets had forgotten his name. The place where he grew up had not even been aware that he was away. He might as well have been in a foreign city, looking for familiar faces, sweet shops, street names. They said he walked around talking to himself, talking to the wide granite slabs underneath his feet, expecting the railings to talk back to him at least.

She was in New York at that time. She had her writer's room in Manhattan and her speaking engagements, so she was unable to come back to look after him, so they said. She received letters from him. She recognized his quiet handwriting. There was no bitterness in the words, even when he was speaking about his father.

Her brother was like a child. He was unable to sort himself out with accommodation, so she got him an apartment in Dublin. She could afford to do that for him with all her success. She was still hoping that he would pick himself up and become independent. But she was hoping for too much. She drew the line at giving him money, because she was afraid of him ending up like their own mother. So then he went to Noleen asking for money. They told me that Noleen leaves the door of her house open while she's working at the kitchen table writing, all the neighbours say hello to her passing by. It's the way it was when Noleen grew up and there was no need to change any of that, the door was always left open for somebody coming back.

This was long after Úna and Noleen had broken up, they said. Úna got used to being away, travelling on her own and giving talks right across America in places like Aspen. And Noleen always loved her. Noleen loved her so much that when her brother came asking for money she got out every penny she had in her bank account and gave him the lot.

38

Manfred says you can buy everything you want. You can buy every coat. Every perfume. Every television. You can buy shoes made from the eel, he says. They are no more than a strip of skin. It's not true that the eel is ugly, he says. It's not true that the eel will suck a baby's blood and the eel does not milk the cows. People tell lies about the eel, he says. He read quite recently in one of the papers that KaDeWe are selling eel-skinned shoes and that people pay a lot of money for them, a Russian woman bought three pairs without even trying them on.

Úna says she has no intention of looking at eel-skinned shoes.

Everything you want is there, Manfred says.

And sheets?

Yes. Every sheet.

She loved the warm air of KaDeWe blasting towards you as you went inside, like arriving on holidays. She loved the height of the ceilings. She loved the spotlights shining on the merchandise like a stage lit up, ready for the actors to come out and speak. She loved the display of fountain pens and watches for men. She loved seeing people going up and down the escalators, standing still, crossing over each other.

She got one of the men at the perfume counter to spray perfume on a card for her and she let him know the smell reminded her of women at the horse show dressed in big hats with chewy sweets in their handbags, or Glacier Mints. She said she loved to do that whenever she had the time, at home or anywhere else in the world, she smelled the perfume they sold. Not to buy it. Only for the chance to talk, really. She said she used go into the toilets of Brown Thomas in Dublin and get a free squirt of perfume on the way out before going to the pub.

Come on, she said. Let's ask the man in the uniform.

She got me to push her out to the lobby again to ask the man with the top hat where to find the sheets. She said she wanted to give him a function and one of these days he'll be retired and they won't replace him, she said, too many people probably just walk past him as if he doesn't exist, even though he's dressed in tails and a top hat, like he's at a wedding, or at the races. He told us what level we needed to go to. She said people can be a bit blind in a department store, they would walk right past their own mother and father. She stopped for a while to watch a woman wearing a black headscarf buying a pink handbag without looking at herself in the mirror, only lifting it up to smell the leather and asking her husband if it suited her, as if he was the mirror.

She said you buy something and it's not the same thing when you get home. You bring something home and it's the last thing you wanted. She said she loved the smell of new leather especially. She said everybody is a child in a department store.

The shop assistant spoke in English, how can I be of assistance to you? She liked to give the shop assistant a chance to tell her what they had in stock, what was to be recommended. You can't go and buy a sheet, she said, without allowing the assistant to show you some of the different fabrics. You don't have to worry about wasting time because they love to tell you what's most comfortable. They can usually guess what kind of sheets you need by the way you look. Cotton. Linen. Satin. The assistant pointed to various brands and designs and also explained the different levels of quality and sheen in the fabric. They had all kinds of patterns. Black and white stripes. Diagonal stripes. Half green with yellow frogs and half yellow with green frogs. Leopardskin sheets. Sheets with the head of a zebra in the middle. Sheets with the alphabet. Sheets with red and yellow leaves tumbling down. Some of the beds were made up already and you felt like getting straight into them, no matter how many people were walking around looking at you asleep.

While she was examining different patterns, her bag was left abandoned in the middle of the floor, like a see-through bag that belonged to nobody.

The shop assistant was a tall woman. She crouched

down beside the wheelchair holding out one pair of sheets after another. She allowed time for her to feel the fabric in her hands. The assistant said sometimes a colour feels warmer than plain white, even though it's only an illusion that people have built up in their minds.

Whatever gives you the best sleep, the assistant said.

Úna said writers don't sleep. She was an insomniac. The only time she ever slept properly in her whole life was when she was writing a novel. The truth keeps you up at night, she said. Fiction makes you sleep.

The assistant said silk sheets are the most beautiful to touch, and the most expensive, of course. But for me, personally, the assistant said, they are very delicate. If you catch your nail or snag a piece of jewellery, that's the end, you can say goodbye to the sheets because the thread will run free.

The assistant spoke like a man and kneeled down like a woman, with her knees together. When the assistant went away to get out more and more sheets, Úna wanted to know my opinion.

Do you think she has an apple?

The assistant?

She has a deep voice, don't you think?

She said a man or a woman like that will always give himself away, like we all give ourselves away. We always leave some small piece of information out for people to find, like something accidentally dropped for somebody to pick up after us. It's not like a woman to cough at that angle, up towards the ceiling, she said, with the apple showing. And maybe that was the whole intention, dropping a clue, letting people know that you are a man pretending to be a woman. Or a woman pretending to be a man. Or a woman pretending to be a woman.

These are the some of the finest sheets we have, the assistant said, coming back with sheets made in France. Or maybe it was Switzerland. They have the quality mark, they will last for ten years, minimum.

Ten years?

Longer, the assistant said.

I don't need them that long, she said. She was bringing them home to Dublin and the assistant said she understood, Ireland.

For the big sleep.

The best sleep, the assistant said.

The last sleep.

Ach, the assistant said.

It was only afterwards that she asked me if I knew what the assistant said. What does *Ach* mean? Because the word *Ach* is the Irish for But. And I knew that the word *Ach* is also the German for Ah.

Ah what?

She bought only the one sheet, one double sheet. Satin. Plain white. No pillows. The assistant asked about measurements but she said it was just for herself and they allowed for an overhang. The assistant wrapped the sheet in a parcel, with a ribbon. The assistant thanked us like a man and smiled like a woman and coughed like a man with her hand over her mouth.

39

We had time to spare. She wanted to look at some
other things. Things we didn't need, like kitchen
utensils, pots and sets of cutlery. Ceramic knives that
she found interesting, and white ceramic frying pans.
Imagine doing sausages in that, she said. She went
around admiring things, touching everything. She
turned to me like a mother and asked me if there
was anything I wanted to bring back with me, but
I couldn't think of anything. Honestly. Surely there
was something I could do with. A shirt, maybe. A
new jacket, something for the wedding. I told her I
was all sorted out with my suit. And anyway, the
wedding was not even happening. It's been called
off, I told her.

Liam, she said. Do you never buy anything?

I laughed.

You never go to the opera and you never buy any
decent clothes, you wear clothes that make you look
like an overgrown teenager. Look at that jacket you
have on, it's like something a soccer player would
have worn about ten years ago.

It's kind of stuck to me now, I said.

In the children's department she was looking at summer dresses. She had to let an assistant know that she was only looking, only having a look, she said, pointing at her eyes.

Then she started asking me questions again, if I knew who Maeve's real father was. The biological father. Is it who I think it is?

Yes, I said.

Are you certain?

He was my best friend, I said.

You never told me that, Liam.

I'm only trying to figure this out now, I said.

He used to call for me all the time. We'd go out drinking together, let's do some damage, he would say, you never knew where it would end up. He was very generous, I told her. He was so generous you would have to say it was overpowering, something you'd nearly be afraid of. I always had the feeling that I was in debt to him. He was great fun, no question. Everybody loved him. He would turn up at the door without warning, smiling, saying *Ra Ra*. The same two words every time. *Ra Ra*. I can't remember ever having a real conversation with him. He preferred everything to be erased. Maybe that's what I liked so much about him, there was no obligation to remember, only to forget. Never look back, he said to me many times. Always walk away. I knew why Emily wanted to escape. Emily had good reasons to ask me to take her away, anywhere away. That's why I brought her to Milltown Malbay and the seaweed baths and all that swimming in the

212

Pollock Holes and lying on the cliffs to make sure we were not being followed.

How could he remain my friend?

He disappeared as soon as Maeve was born. I thought I was bound to run into him somewhere, sooner or later. Dublin is a small place. The odds were in favour of me seeing him in one of the bars we used to go into. Somewhere, waiting at the traffic lights. Maybe getting a take-away coffee. I told her I saw him once in the foyer at the Abbey Theatre. No, at a concert, I think it was, the Olympia. Long ago. This was well before I found out that I was not Maeve's biological father. I walked right up to him and put my hand on his shoulder and said how's tricks? Which was a stupid thing to say, I fully agree. How's tricks? I don't know anyone who says that any more, only that he used to say that to me all the time and that's where I got it from. And anyway, it wasn't him. I was mistaken, it was somebody else.

He's keeping out of your way now, she said.

He might be at the reunion.

Maybe you should go, she said. Clear the air.

She held a child's party dress across her lap and spread it out over her knees with her hands, as if she was going to be wearing it.

I told her I sent him a letter, to his home address. I didn't think it was right to send an email or leave a message on his phone. I didn't want to send anything to his office either in case his secretary might open it.

What does he do?

Strictly private and confidential, I said, that's what I wrote at the top of the envelope.

You don't have to tell me, she said.

Of course, I said. He's a barrister.

I told her it was a very polite letter. I didn't accuse him of being the father or anything like that, because I have no definite proof, do I? I didn't even link him to Maeve. I congratulated him on his success in the legal world and told him about my daughter having trouble finding her biological father. I think I might have made it sound a bit like a legal letter. I asked him if he could think back and remember anything that might help Maeve locate her real father, if he had any information that might be helpful, that is, then I would be very grateful to hear from him.

And did you?

No.

Maybe he never got it.

She had no intention of buying a dress for a five-year-old girl. She only remembered spilling red lemonade on her favourite dress once and she always wanted to buy the same dress again for the rest of her life.

I told her it was a mistake to send the letter. I was angry with myself for sending it. Angry with myself for letting him know and angry with him for taking my daughter away from me. I wanted to reverse all that, but you can't, can you? You can't just knock on somebody's door and demand a letter back. You can't walk into somebody's house and say excuse me, you were not meant to know that. You were not the intended recipient.

You wouldn't do that, she said.

Out in the country, I said. Near Trim. That's where

he lives now. It's a bit hard to find at first, the sat-nav sends you all around the world. Beautiful place, with a long driveway and lawns and a tennis court. He has two stone greyhounds on either side of the front door, covered with yellow lichen. There's a fanlight over the door. The front room is full of bookshelves, wall to wall. A painting of a field of wheat after a storm over the mantelpiece. And the kitchen has black and white tiles, diagonal.

How do you know all that, she asked.

Imagine if I let myself in the back door, I said, through the kitchen. Imagine if I walked right up the stairs. The two of them sitting up in bed, him and his wife. Him reading some legal journal and her reading what? Poetry? And me appearing out of nowhere, in the door of the bedroom. If you don't mind, I need that piece of information back. About my daughter. Pretend you never heard it.

You didn't, Liam.

You couldn't do that, I said. She would puke all over herself with the fright, so she would. She would puke all over the book and the duvet. And him saying, it's OK Julia, it's only a friend of mine from school I haven't seen in years.

You're not going to do that, Liam.

I'm different now, I said.

When I'm gone, she said.

I swear, I'm not like that any more.

And then I saw myself in the mirror. At first I thought there was somebody watching me. Maybe security personnel, checking me out. But it was nothing more than a mirror in front of me and I was standing there live, in person, not recognizing myself.

It was the shoes I noticed first. They were just like mine, I thought, only a bit more shabby-looking in a place where everything was new. And the trousers, bunched up over the shoes. I looked second-hand. I was in my own world, a bit lost, maybe, not sure if I was in the right place, that kind of expression. I could see myself in all honesty, nothing hidden, the way other people see me. I was not being anyone but myself. I recognized the nose, the crooked nose, more broken in reverse. I could see for the first time how I ended up. This is what I had ended up looking like, this reflection, standing in a department store in Berlin with a parcel under my arm and a sheet inside. I looked found-out.

40

They want to know if there was anything more I found out about Úna. While I was in Berlin. As if I had the missing clue. Something about her I was keeping to myself, some tiny detail she left behind that would reveal who she really was. But who am I to describe her life? We were just good friends, don't forget. I was her companion, not her lover, we had no previous history between us.

All I can say is read her books, that's who she was. That's her story, in her own words, you can't get better than that. Talk to the people who loved her. Talk to Noleen. Talk to the men in her life. Talk to her family, her friends, the people she worked with, the people who know her better than I do. The only thing I can add is that she loved travelling. I brought her to Berlin and she loved every single minute, that's what she said. She didn't want to stop, she said she was having the time.

What am I trying to say? I can give you a kind of summary of what I know, but it's nothing like meeting her, hearing her speaking for herself. So maybe that's the missing clue? Her presence. Her being alive. A memoir is not a living person, no matter how true it is, that's what I'm trying to say. I know this goes against her opinion that everybody is the sum of their own story and people are nothing more than walking stories, but I don't know if putting together what she told me is ever going to match listening to her live, in her own voice.

She was the kind of person who was no good at inventing things. She preferred real facts. She liked to be at the centre of the facts herself. That's how she wrote her books, putting down a list of facts, first-hand. And sometimes she got the truth mixed up with the facts. She thought you had to tell all the facts to tell the truth. She said some facts were so true you couldn't make them up and some facts were so true they spoke for themselves.

She didn't know how to keep things to herself. She was the kind of person who spoke to everyone in the street. She usually took the leaflet for the free pizza offer and she would sign the petition for an environmental impact study and stop to say hello to the man with two dogs, the man singing 'Angie' on a portable amplifier. Whatever city she was in, she got people talking about themselves, because she knew only too well what it's like when people pretend you don't exist. And sometimes she was in too much of a hurry and there was no time for any of that, taking notice of people. And the thing she hated most was somebody you had already given money to coming back two minutes later as if they had never seen you before.

She was full of anger, plenty of it. She would be the first to admit that herself, we can all be like that from time to time. She could be jealous and hurt and those things people feel in the course of their lives, afraid of others doing better, more money, more successful, women more beautiful. She was on the side of women and she was also afraid of women. She stood up for women and she was jealous of them. She would walk over any women in the world to take a man away from a woman. She was straight and she was gay. She turned in every direction for love.

She loved bells. At one point, while we were driving through Berlin, she wanted to listen to the bells. She sat forward suddenly and told Manfred to stop the car, I thought there was something wrong. Manfred, she shouted, stop the car, this minute. Here. Stop, right here, anywhere, she said. So Manfred had to pull in at the nearest loading bay so that she could roll down the window to let the bells in.

We were right next to the church and it was deafening, you couldn't hear a thing. It was like a roof closing down on the city, the bells were gone mad. They were furious, so it seemed to me. Even the traffic going by was silent. Manfred switched off the engine and we sat there and listened, like New Year's Eve. You could feel the bells more than hear them. Actually, we realized that we were also hearing other bells from other churches farther away. The bells had some kind of harmony going. Maybe not so much a harmony but the sound of each bell layered on top of the other, humming in our ears. And the thing was this, when the bells stopped ringing, they didn't really stop. We continued hearing them as they were fading away, like somebody getting his breath back.

She was not the kind of person who went into churches much. She had no time for God, only that she couldn't get out of the habit of using God as an expression. God Almighty. God help us. She didn't see the point in God, but she still wanted her funeral to be held in a church and she still wanted to go into the church left in ruins, it was on the itinerary which Manfred had on the dashboard, to light a candle for her brother.

And after all that she said about her brother, she still could not help but admire her father. She loved it when people came up to her and said she was her father's daughter. And when he died, there was such a big funeral for him, as big as her own funeral, because he was so well loved, he was the king. She was in bits after his death and started drinking like her mother. She said she didn't see any point in drinking unless you drank too much. As a child she was used to people coming home drunk at night. Every time somebody came in late she expected them to be drunk, crashing into things, laughing or angry. She said she would never forgive her father for any of that, and still when she heard his voice on the radio it tore the lungs straight out of her chest. She tried to talk to her mother but her mother was always too drunk to listen. She found her mother often collapsed on the floor and she was left banging on the window, thinking she was dead. And then one day her mother was found dead, lying face down on the bathroom floor with all the bruises from previous falls.

At one point, Úna was driving out to the west and she realized you could switch off your own emotions like a car radio. It was like hearing nothing. Like being underwater. She discovered how to live her own life and pursue her own happiness instead of worrying about her family.

It was a bit of a surprise arriving at the church in ruins because there was so little to see. All there was left was the broken steeple, as if the war had only happened the other day. We went in and saw the shell of the church from inside, only the mosaic ceiling in one part still intact, quite well preserved, with a few cracks running through it. We saw pictures taken of the church before the war when it was still standing and nobody could have had any idea how the place would look in ruins after the war. Imagine not knowing, she said. And right beside the ruins was the new church, built as a replacement, a modern octagonal shape made up of small blue windows or blue stained pieces of glass, like a million blue squares with light coming through. So the whole church was full of blue light. It was like being inside a blue vase, no matter what the weather was like outside it was always full of blue light, blue across the floor, blue across the benches, blue across our faces.

At the door, there was a basket of apples, so you could give a donation to the church and take an apple. There was a drawing of the Madonna that she wanted to see, an oval shape of a mother wrapped around a child, keeping it warm, drawn in charcoal on the back of a street map of Stalingrad during the war.

At the candle-stand there was a small steel container attached to a chain, with a slot for the money at the top. The coins made a clinking sound as I threw them in. The tray had real candles, naked flame, not like in some churches where you pay for an electric light flickering, low voltage. So I lit a candle for her brother, Jimmy. Then I placed it into an empty space on the tray and we looked at it for a while.

I asked her was there anyone else? Did she want to light one for her parents maybe?

One for your mother and father, I said.

No, she said.

She wanted no candle lit for her mother and father, absolutely not, only her brother. It was hopeless trying to persuade her to forgive, because you could never forgive something that was done to another person, she said, only something that was done to yourself.

I'm not entitled to forgive what was done to my brother, she said.

Her brother was only a child at the time, she said. He saw what was going on. He told her what happened, in letters. He wrote to her, putting it all down on paper as though he could give the memory away to her for safe-keeping. He wrote telling her what he remembered, because she was the writer in the family and she would know what to do with the information. She carried that information with her all over the world, the story of her brother became part of her own story. And even though it was all told in her books, it was still impossible for him to get rid of the noise that remained inside his head. Ever since he was a small boy, he carried that sound like a companion walking beside him, whispering in his ear. What he witnessed would never stop, even though his mother and father were both long gone now. No matter how many letters he wrote, the memory would always belong to him.

He was at the mercy, she said.

He heard his mother was calling for help. He heard the sound of his father's fist. He heard the sound of his mother's face. He heard the love leaving his mother at night and never coming back, there was nothing he could do to help her. And then he hid himself in a drawer. He was not much more than four years old at the time and he was trying to get away from what he heard, they found him asleep in the drawer of the wardrobe next morning.

41

Would it make a difference if I had been able to tell her about the future, how things turn out? I would love to have told her that I've come back here to Berlin and the church with the blue light is still the same, no difference. The same blue squares of glass all around and the blue sunlight entering through them, spreading evenly across everyone who comes in. You get the impression that your hands are turning blue and silent, remembering. You come out into the brightness of the street with your blue fingers sensitive to the noise of traffic. Time has moved on a good bit into the autumn now, I would love to tell her. The city has kept going, moving ahead of you and it's changed colour again to brown and copper and red and everything in between. Leaves curled up and crunching under your feet. Leaves spread out along the path in the park, men and women making great piles of them with wide rakes. I would love her to have seen the way the city looks at this time. Leaves in the shop windows, hanging, falling around the display of writing materials, handpicked leaves in unbelievable colours like blood red and yellow as flame, some of them still holding on to green at the edges, in among pens and diaries and leather-bound photo albums.

And lanterns.

I would love her to have seen the lanterns. One evening when I was coming through the park and it was already dark, I want to tell her, I saw about ten or fifteen of them gathered in an open space. Other lanterns came out from the trees around the edge of the park to join in with them. They were mostly orange, but other colours as well. It made me think of a luminous underwater creature, shifting and changing shape constantly. That's how I would describe it to her. And then I saw that they were all mothers and fathers with children. Some of the lanterns turned out to be faces lit up by lanterns. One of the lanterns broke away and started moving quickly up a small hill with another lantern after it. Until they both came back and joined in with the main group again. Then the entire collection of lanterns began moving very slowly towards me. There must have been about thirty or forty of them in all, I would say, getting closer and closer until I was surrounded by lanterns, all singing as they passed me by.

That would have been good for her to see.

I would love to have told her some more optimistic things. Would that have made a difference to the way she thought of me, the general impression that she took away with her at the end of her life?

Your daughter will be all right, she said to me.

It's good to remember her saying that. She was guessing at the future in her absence, telling me not to worry so much, things would take care of themselves, you can't plan out everything in advance. As regards what she thought of me, I don't know. She was free to assume anything she liked, she had that gift. And I could no more influence her view of me than I can influence what other people think of me. It's not in my hands to shape the story that people remember.

All I could think of telling her in Berlin was that my brother continues to keep the house where we grew up intact, the same front door, the same windows, everything unchanged. The pictures, the books, the hallway table, even the mice running along the floor, they still have the same entry-point under the stairs. If I was living there, I told her, I might have ripped everything out including the old plumbing, that's me, I have the tendency to renovate. My brother is happy to live with his childhood around him.

Everything is there, I told her. The view overlooking the back gardens, the apple trees, the granite walls with the snails hiding in the ivy, the back gate that never closed properly. Even the sky is unchanged, still shaking with the bang of my father's fist on the table. And the sash window that broke one night in a storm. My father came rushing into the bedroom full of anger and I thought he was coming to punish me, but he was only coming to close the window, which was rattling. It was the days of wood and putty, the sash frame was rotten, and when he tried to close it down, the bottom of the frame came apart in his hands like a piece of fruit cake. The glass was smashed. My father had to find a way to cover the gaps, so he switched on the light and looked around the room for the nearest thing at hand. In the corner of the room there was an old atlas, a big rolled-up school atlas which he kept from the time he was a schoolteacher in Dunmanway. He rolled it out and nailed it up against the window frame. It's a temporary solution, he said. Go to sleep. So that's how I fell asleep, looking at the world from my bed, with my back against the wall. All the anger was outside. The branches of the trees throwing shadows onto the world and the wind flapping across the oceans.

I never thought it was possible to live without anger in Ireland. Maybe my father was also like the King in *Don Carlo*. He was full of love and guilt and fear of losing his power. But he was not trying to kill me. He was just very sensitive to noise, that's all. Even the phone would make him jump. I don't know what made him like that, maybe he was still listening out for all the things that scared him, things from his own childhood perhaps, his own father missing. He was scared by the noise of children. It was like something he couldn't fix, like water hammer. He didn't know what to do with children making noise. And the only thing you could do with water hammer was to rip out the whole plumbing system and start again from scratch. He loved children in his own way. He was good at remembering birthdays. He was good at buying mouth organs and geography magazines and teaching the rules of chess. But he couldn't take any of us running around the house, bouncing on beds or jumping down three steps at the bottom of the stairs, it would make him leap up from his chair and the book would fly out of his hand, we were worse than water hammer.

She made me work things out for myself. It's only in Berlin with her that I discovered how to remember, how time was always going backwards in our family. I was a child watching, like her, unable to explain it until I went back and began to remember the same things as my brother.

Why was it so difficult for my father's brother to come and visit my mother? And why was my mother so unhappy about him not coming? I didn't understand why anyone would want a visit from somebody who remained so silent, somebody whose silence was so terrifying. Now I think of the Jesuit and his silence more as a quiet aggression in the house. Withholding words. Saying nothing seems worse than saying the worst. It's only now that I understand how it was exactly this silence in my father's brother that my mother admired so much. After my father died, she sat looking out the window at the gardens unchanged, waiting for him, the Jesuit. But he was in love with my aunt. The Jesuit was unable to visit because my aunt was afraid he still loved my mother. Because my father's brother and my mother had so much to remember together. Every baptism, every communion, every time we were sick with asthma and he came up the stairs and silently made the sign of the cross over us so we could breathe again. Every time he came to pray for better school results, every time there was a problem in the house between me and my father and the Jesuit had to come and act as a mediator, only that he never said a word, just kept his silence.

There was great excitement whenever my father's brother came to see us. My mother made us put on our best clothes, she put the best table-cloth on the table, she made the best cake and she quickly took off her apron when she heard the bell ringing. My father's brother brought sweets in his pocket, and books, and silence. Silence that made my father jealous. Books that made him suspicious. My father insisted on reading all the books first, to see what was in them, what his brother might be saying to my mother through these books. My father loved my mother through music and my father's brother loved her through books. And then my father's brother fell in love with my aunt. He continued living under one roof with the Jesuits, but he was more often staying under the same roof with my aunt. He no longer came to visit my mother, he couldn't.

I don't know what my father thought about all this at the time. I have never tried to imagine what was going on inside his head. His mind was not a place we were allowed into either, because he never showed us how he felt, only with his anger. I'm not even sure I have the right to enter now and specu-late over my father's thoughts, because he left so little for us to go on. I can remember nothing that he ever said about his brother, not a single word. I think he was like us, afraid of his brother, the Jesuit. I think my father loved my mother so much he was afraid of her talking to anyone else, even us. Most of all, I think he was afraid of the Jesuit. He was afraid he could never match his brother's silence.

Apart from that I have no idea what he was thinking. I'm just standing in for him now, as a father.

He took us out fishing one day around that time, I remember, myself and my brother, we caught lots of mackerel and my father left a smile behind him in the boat. Or was it a smile? Maybe it was only the sun in his eyes and the effort of rowing. My brother and I both remember this word for word, my father smiling with his eyes closed and the oars squeaking, the water dripping from the oars faster than honey dripping from the spoon, and my brother was trying to slow the boat down with his hand in the water. We remember that day in exactly the same order – my father's hands tying up the wet rope to the rusted ring in the harbour wall, the fine spray of water springing from the rope when it was tightened, the salt on our hands, the mackerel in a plastic bag still jumping and shivering inside. We were standing on the pier very hungry, our stomachs empty after coming back in off the sea, and my father was saying that he would bring us straight up for chips.

And maybe that's why our memory is so aligned on this. Because it was the biggest surprise hearing my father say we were going for chips. As if he stopped being our father and he was going to be more like other fathers from then on. We looked at each other standing on the pier and wondered what changed him. We thought he had suddenly turned into the best father in the world. He was not the kind of man who ever bought chips, he was against all that take-away food. He wanted people to eat their food where it was cooked, where they bought it. Because our house was exactly the distance of a packet of chips away from the chipper. People coming home from the pub at night always arrived right outside our house as they finished their fish and chips, so they threw the empty wrapper into our front garden. My father said they treated our garden like a refuse bin. And sometimes he stood at the bedroom window, installed like a security camera, just to see it for himself. Every Monday morning he would go out and put all the discarded chip papers from the weekend into the bin, then he came inside to wash his hands. Once we heard him say that he was going to collect all the empty chip bags and bring them back to the chipper at the end of the year. Sometimes people threw the packet of chips into our garden even before they finished eating them and we lay in our beds thinking about the uneaten chips inside. Our garden was the cut-off point and nobody ate chips any further beyond that because they were normally gone cold by then. My father hated anything to do with chips. He hated anything to do with salt and vinegar. It's hard to explain what made him change his mind and break all his own rules, give in, go against his own principles. Myself and my brother talk about that day

231

and we both believe my father wanted to find out once and for all what the truth was. He wanted to find out if our house really was the exact distance of a packet of chips. So he bought chips for himself and one each for me and my brother. And it took as long to get home as it took to eat the chips.

42

We covered a lot of ground together in Berlin. In time, in words, in the things we said to each other, in the places we went to visit. She had not come to Berlin to see the place and go away again like a tourist. She wanted more than that. She had come looking for something in herself, I knew that. Something left unsaid. Some clue dropped in the streets. I mean, how much information is enough? When can you say you really know a city? Or a person? When can you say that you know yourself?

She was not mad about Sanssouci. We were out there briefly and she couldn't wait to move on, it was stifling, all that opulence. She said the palace was designed like a wedding cake and she had no time for that sort of thing. On the way back she wanted to stop at the Wannsee Villa, where the Wannsee Conference took place. She came out silent.

We passed by the old airport where the Americans rescued the people of West Berlin. We saw the synagogue with the golden dome. We saw the Turkish vegetable shops and Manfred showed her the street where he was living. We saw a house that was not renovated yet, with peeling paint along the façade and balconies with junk left out on them. Bicycles. Slogans written up about freedom and justice, words that didn't completely make sense, like free all prisoners. An end to all money. Stuff that people think up late at night. She loved that, people thinking outside the normal way of life. People with a bit of artistic rage left in them, she said. We saw an old wooden door with so much graffiti on it that it must have felt like walking into an abstract painting, like living inside a work of art. And outside on the pavement there were lots of things thrown out, a TV and a used mattress, bits of broken furniture, a sofa waiting to be sat on, an old reading lamp, bits of living without the lives.

The city is a contradiction, she said to me.

And she was a contradiction too, she was the first to admit. It's my life and I have the right to contradict myself. I'm a big, random life, full of messy contradictions, that's what she said. And at some point all the contradictions in a person fit together into one life. The contradictions are not contradictions any more, they become the story. Like all the contradictions come together in one city.

If there was a clue to describe who she really was, then maybe it was something in herself that was always missing. Some place inside that could not be reached. Something that remained unresolved, put on hold. She said she had the weather inside her, changing all the time. Her life was a mixed-up condition, so she said, swinging between sadness and happiness, between loving everything and regretting everything.

She told me about one of the great moments in her life. The time when they were travelling in Italy together. Herself and Noleen. Along the coast. Going by the side of the cliffs, on a train, through the tunnels. Every now and again the carriage was thrown into darkness. From what she was saying it was probably not unlike the end of the day and when they came out of the tunnel it was a new day beginning, I know that feeling. The view of the sea bursting into the carriage again. She said it was hard to look, it was blinding, your eyes would start watering with all the brightness. They were alone in the carriage together, with the window wide open and the breeze blowing in, flapping at their hair, at their light summer clothes.

They had only one book to read on the train, she told me. Noleen and myself, she said, we had an argument over who was going to read it first. I won the toss because I was the faster reader and it was me who brought the book in the first place, she said. But then Noleen started distracting me, looking out the window and making remarks in her deep voice, making me laugh. In fact Noleen decided to sing a song. Thank God there was nobody listening, she said, whatever it was. I'm glad it was not Bob Dylan. At least I hope she was not singing 'Girl from the North Country', she said. We did that as a duet together sometimes, we murdered it. Noleen could do Johnny Cash with her deep voice, and I did Bob Dylan, because I couldn't sing at all.

Noleen was like a big sister, she said, making me laugh in spite of myself, reminding me that there was more to life than the characters in a book. So you know what we did, Úna said. After I read each page I tore it out and passed it over to her.

That's how we read the novel, she said. Every time I finished a page I ripped it out and Noleen read it. And when she was finished reading it she put each page neatly down on the seat beside her. At one point, coming out of a tunnel, she said, a gust of wind came into the carriage like an invisible hand, like the hand of the next reader impatiently grabbing the pages off the seat and pulling them out the window in no sequence at all. Some of the pages flew down towards the cliffs, she said. Some of them went up vertically, up over the roof of the train. Some of them flew along the length of the train, attempting to get back on again, trying some of the doors and windows further down. Honestly, she said, they looked like birds. White birds with writing on them. An entire novel full of birds left behind along that journey.

What was the book?

I can't tell you that, she said.

What was it about?

I'm not sure I can remember too much of what was in it, she said.

She could only remember the pages flying. Then the train stopped. We were held up somewhere along the coast, she said, miles away from anywhere, with the sounds of clicking and snapping in the metal underneath. I'll never forget it, she said, as long as I live. Only the two of us alone inside the compartment and the heat and the breeze coming in from the sea across both open windows. Nobody came to tell us anything or explain why we were stopped. Over three hours the train was unable to move because of a forest fire ahead. We could smell the smoke in the carriage, she said. We were stuck in time. Everything on hold. Two women, she said, left behind on a train overlooking the Adriatic. Staring at the blue sea. And the terns diving. The terns squeaking and diving, like pages from the book, she said, because they changed direction so fast.

43

I told her what happened with my daughter. Úna wanted to know all that, about Maeve going to see her real father. I told her how she had been trying to contact him, the biological father, but he refused to get back to her.

Think about this clearly, I said to Maeve. He's not going to get back to you, that's guaranteed. And there is nothing to be gained by going to see him in his house, I said, only more trouble. Think about what's important, Maeve, I said. Think about the good things, like I try to remember good things about my own father. Remember the time you wanted to be a unicorn for Halloween, I said. A golden unicorn. The trouble it took to make that outfit before you changed your mind at the last minute and wanted to be an angel instead, so I had to find wings somewhere quickly. I don't know if Maeve remembers a lot of those things, only me reminding her.

You can't plan what a child is going to remember. Maeve was very cool about all this. I've never seen her more confident. She put her hands around my face and called me Dad and said this was only something she had to do for herself, she used the word identity.

She knew what he looked like, her biological father. She had pictures downloaded off the net. Photos of him at conferences in America, Germany, Cairo and places like that. Looking really well, I have to say. The same as ever. Serious, afraid of nobody, but also up for a laugh as always. His hair is a different colour now, darker than I remember. Only his moustache is the same colour as before.

She tried to make an appointment to see him, but he was unavailable. His secretary was protecting him, so I gather, from people not referred to him by other legal practices, people coming to him with private matters, unsolicited, if you like. So then Maeve decided to go in there, into the courts, in person. It's a public place, she's perfectly entitled to be there as much as anyone else.

Maeve found out where he was likely to be. She's that type of person, I said, just like her mother, quite determined. She went there and examined all the lawyers standing around, waiting for the court to be in session. Trying to identify her father.

Her biological father, Úna said.

Yes, that's right, I said. And then she found him. He was standing in a group, she recognized him straight away, no mistake, dressed in a suit, with a black gown loosely draped around his shoulders. Maeve said he had a look of calmness, a single-minded expression, full of concentration. He was accepting a file from somebody and nodding, or half bowing, slowly, to say thank you. He was shaking hands with one or two of the other lawyers and smiling. She saw him leaning his head down to listen to somebody whispering some last-minute information into his ear.

She walked right up and apologized for interrupting him, but she would like to have a word, she spoke his name.

He didn't react, so Maeve told me. She repeated herself, giving her own name this time. It's Maeve, she said to him. She didn't say the word daughter, she had no intention of embarrassing him. But he was in preparation mode for the trial. He turned away from her. He had no time to be distracted by things that were long in the past now and as much forgotten as they could be.

He didn't hear, Úna said.

He must have heard, I said. Everyone else heard. You know when your name has been called. There has to be a little tug, when the voice that says something connects with the ear that hears it, don't you think?

How could he not hear?

Then she spoke her mother's name, I said. Emily.

And that made him turn around. He looked at Maeve and studied her face very carefully. He must have thought he had suddenly gone back in time and he was seeing Emily in front of him, a miniature Emily with the same lips and the same smile, the hair, same everything about her. He must have thought he had stopped in time also, not a day older than he was with Emily. He stepped towards her and shook her hand, then led her away from the group he was with. He said he was pushed for time, could he get back to her.

If you leave your number with my secretary, he said to her.

I've already done that, Maeve said.

That's good, he said. I'll be in touch with you.

I can always come back here, Maeve said. If I don't hear from you.

He said nothing more, just smiled. I suppose he liked that in her, she was just like Emily, not going to be swept away by excuses. So that's the way it was left. She smiled at him and pulled her hair back like she was opening the curtains. Then she turned and walked away.

I thought Maeve only wanted to lay eyes on him, I said. She wanted to see what he looked like in real life. She wanted to say his name. She wanted to see her reflection, that's all, I thought.

I know they've met since then, I told Úna. She's met her real father. She's been out to his house, I have no problem with that. It's not like a competition any more. Maeve is not comparing fathers, only exercising her right to know. She told me what his house looked like, the greyhounds guarding the front door with yellow lichen on their faces. She described the fanlight over the door, and the front room with the oak bookcases and the painting of a wheat field with the angle of the sunlight low. Maeve was shown around the rooms, the bedrooms with the books on the bedside tables. She met his wife,

Julia. The kitchen is huge, with black and white diagonal tiles and there's an island in the middle, double sink, a professional-level gas cooker with six rings. He loves cooking apparently, could have been a master chef, anything he put his mind down to. He looked very fit, so Maeve told me. He was wearing a tracksuit. He offered her a drink and they sat for a while in the living room together. She told me that he was sitting at one end of the room and she was sitting at the other end, at far ends, if you like, with a wide rug between them because the room was so large.

44

I had no more follow-on news to give Úna in Berlin. I wish I could have told her that we had fine weather for the wedding, everything went well, it was a great day. I wish I could have told her that my daughter was very happy, expecting a baby. I wish I could have told her all kinds of good news about the world that has not even happened yet.

I gave her my wedding speech.

That's all I had at the time. I asked Úna if I could try it out on her. I told her that if my daughter ever got married, I was all ready with the speech. Could I rehearse it with her, I said, because she was not going to make the wedding anyway, even if it was happening after all.

It's the usual father's speech, I said. The one that every father makes. I'm sure they've all heard it before. About a taxi driver coming to the door of the house at four in the morning, asking if I could come out to the car and identify my daughter. Was that my daughter asleep in the back of his cab? And did I have any way of waking her up, because he didn't want to shake her, physically, and he had tried everything including Jethro Tull full volume, he had been a taxi driver for thirty years, it never failed before. Absolutely, I said to him. No doubt whatsoever, it was my daughter, Maeve. I was her father, I said a few times, always was. The taxi driver looked as if he was suddenly in doubt and he had come to the wrong house, but then I paid him the fare and carried her in. I was the world expert at carrying a sleeping child in from the car, all the way into bed without waking her up. I was able to do it without letting her head roll back, bending down to open doors with one hand, making sure not to pass with her face directly under the light, pulling back the sheets even. I had lots of practice over the years. I managed to transfer her in from the taxi and lay her out on the bed, but then she woke up, just after I got her shoes off and covered her up. Maeve sat up wondering where she was, asking if there were any rashers, she could murder a rasher sandwich, with mayonnaise.

I know every father says they have that story, but it's mine.

The problem was, there were no rashers. I checked in the fridge and found nothing. You know how it is, nobody went shopping and the fridge was empty. There was not even sliced bread for toast, as far as I remember. So I decided to make chips. I knew she would like that, home-made chips. So I started peeling potatoes. She came down in her dressing gown and slippers and sat at the table watching me. It was the summer, I remember, the beginning of brightness was already coming in through the window. I was asking her questions, how the night went. General questions that you ask as a father, not really expecting any answers, did you have a good time? She smiled at me, but she was saying nothing. We had no deep fryer, only a pot and the bottle of vegetable oil from the last time I made chips, so it still had sediments of burnt potato at the bottom. I cut the potatoes into chips and dried them indi-vidually on a fresh kitchen towel. The oil was making hot squeaking sounds and it started bubbling up as soon as I dropped the chips in. It's a lovely sight, I thought to myself, boiling oil. I felt like the man in the chipper, with people watching me, waiting for their chips. I put on the extractor fan so it was hard to talk. I was asking Maeve more and more ques-tions, fishing for information, I suppose. Again she smiled, tracing a permanent tea stain on the wooden table with her finger, holding her dressing gown closed over with the other hand. Her hair was tied up at the top of her head which made it look like a feather stuck forward. And I was busy concentrating on the chips, lifting them up with a slotted steel spoon to make sure they were not sticking to one another, waiting for them to get crispy and change colour from white to light brown.

This is what I remember. The chips in a bowl on a double layer of kitchen paper and Maeve sprin-kling salt over them, ketchup on the side, eating them even though they were still far too hot, hardly able to hold them in her fingers. She took a small bite, keeping her mouth open as if she was holding on to a piece of information, like volcanic rock, throwing it back and forth, breathing quickly in and out. You know the way, I've often seen people outside the chipper doing this, I've done it myself, I've even seen my own father doing it that one time I remember him buying chips for us, rattling the bag, huffing as if you really want to say something and you can't wait to put it into words, only you have to let the chip in your mouth cool down first and not burn your tongue.

Of course I was not going to put all this into the wedding speech, not all the details. But that's the story as I remember it. I was giving Úna the unabridged version in Berlin, asking her advice, I suppose, trying to see if it works, would they still be interested?

Keep it short, Liam, Úna advised me. The wedding guests don't want to know everything. They'll want to start dancing at that point, if they're still able to stand up.

I laughed.

Get to the point, she said.

I'm not trying to make any point, I said. I'm only saying it felt good to be able to carry Maeve in from the taxi. It felt good to be making chips. It was great seeing my daughter eating the chips with her bare feet on the cross beam of the kitchen table, rocking her chair back.

And then Emily came down the stairs, wearing a similar dressing gown. They looked so alike, Emily and Maeve. They both had the same hair tied up, identical. They looked like they were going for an early-morning swim. Mother and daughter. One swimming ahead of the other. What was going on, Emily wanted to know. Was I making mountains of chips again, in the middle of the night? Yes, we we're having a few chips, I said. Emily sat down at the table and tasted one of the chips and Maeve started talking. Maeve was telling us everything. How she had met somebody, his name was Shane, he makes me laugh a lot, she said, and his family owns a farm in Leitrim with the ruins of an ancient church on their land, all covered in ivy, it would be lovely to get married there, out in the open with no roof.

It was getting bright outside, I could hear the birds. We still had the lights on because it was in between night and next day. I got up to make a few more chips, another batch, why not? I continued listening to Maeve and started peeling more and more potatoes, not knowing when to stop.

45

We should be watching the time. By right we should be heading straight back to the hotel at this point. It's late in the afternoon and I'm not sure she's up to seeing anything now, she can't absorb any more sights. She must be exhausted, there is something going on in her thoughts that she's not letting me know about. I can see it in her eyes, she's worried. And for a day that was quite warm, it's gone quite cold. Getting out of the car you feel it. But she's determined to see the memorial. It's on the list of things she wanted to see, the list I gave Manfred, no question of leaving it out.

At first you think it's not finished yet, like a building site. All these grey blocks or square concrete pillars, columns with a smooth concrete finish. It's not fenced off or anything. You see a few people walking around between the columns and you realize that it's been designed to look like that, empty, unequal, in long lines at different levels, with columns getting taller and deeper and further away, this is what people have come to see.

The sun has gone and the wind is coming straight through. There's no shelter. She won't be able to stand the cold out here for very long, that's what I'm saying to myself. This is going to be very brief, so we leave everything in the car, she won't be needing her bag. I make sure she has her cap on. And why does she not have a scarf?

Manfred is waiting by the car.

There's no official entrance, so you can make your way in from any side you like. Straight into the low columns or straight into the high columns, there's no difference. I push the wheelchair into a row that leads us towards the centre, if there is a centre. The ground is uneven with cobbles. The front wheels rattle and the wheelchair is tilted, like on a rough road. I continue pushing the wheelchair further along the row going down and we're almost underground at this stage, that's the feeling. She wants to stop and look around. There's nobody there. You don't hear anything much. You could be lost and nobody would know. We're talking about a place right in the middle of the city that makes you feel like you could be left behind, deserted. Nothing but lines of grey columns and grey cobbles. And you would expect a bit more shelter down there but the wind is actually stronger, like a wind tunnel, the gap between the columns is pulling the wind from far off and you feel even more exposed.

I thought it was the cold that made her so silent. But she said she didn't feel anything, she was fine. Later on she told me that it made her feel guilty being there. She wouldn't tell me what it was that made her feel guilty, only that she felt guilty and she could not say. It seemed to me that everybody visiting this place was bringing their own guilt with them, leaving it behind in the concrete. This is only something I thought to myself afterwards. It felt as though all the guilt in the world was being brought here, adding to the columns, growing new columns. As if this was the collecting point where all the guilt was going to be kept from now on.

Is silence even a good word for it? I'm not sure. There among the grey columns you could hear all the words that were still calling out to be said. The silence underneath the streets, coming up through the pavement. That's what I was listening to, I think. An entire city full of words not even invented yet coming up to the surface.

It was too cold to speak. So I got her back to the hotel and she wanted to go up to her room alone, I respected that. She wanted to spend some time on her own, without me asking questions. Even when I was not asking questions, my presence was like a conscience walking beside her.

So that's when I went to speak to Manfred and she went upstairs to her room. I gave Manfred the plans for the evening and let him know that we didn't need him any more. I must have been there speaking to Manfred for a couple of minutes, no more. He protested a bit, but then he accepted the instructions given to him and left. And in that short space of time, she had gone up in the elevator. She must have got to the right floor because I had pressed the right number for her and even watched the dial outside going all the way up to the fourth floor. She knew the number of her room, there was no fear of her getting lost.

When I was finished talking to Manfred, I went up to my room. I could understand that she wanted to be alone, but I phoned her room to make sure there was nothing she needed. There was no answer. I went around to knock on her door. She was probably having a rest and I didn't want to disturb her. I walked up and down the corridor and came back to knock again, because it was not like her to ignore me like this without some reason. She should have told me that she was fine, at least, not to worry. And when I was getting no answer, I thought there might have been something wrong, was there some emergency I needed to help her with? I didn't want to start worrying too much, only that hearing nothing made me think the worst. If only she had her mobile I could have contacted her that way, but it was switched off and I had her see-through bag in my hand in any case. I called her room again. There was still no answer, so I went back down to the lobby to see if she had somehow gone down there to look for me. That's the only way I could explain it to myself. I was trying not to assume the worst thing right away. I even checked outside the hotel on the street, in case she went out there to see if I was talking to Manfred by the car, which was gone at that point. I ran back inside and went upstairs once more, banging on the door and shouting this time to see if she was all right in there. All I could think of doing was to go back down to the lobby, into the restaurant, around the hallways, anywhere I thought she might have got lost looking for me. I went to the reception to ask if she had left a message. She had to be in her room. I was sure something had happened to her. She might have fallen, maybe worse. I had no option but to go back to the reception desk and tell them it was an emergency. Not that I wanted to alarm them, only would they mind opening the door of her room, it was stupid of me not to have kept a spare key. This took a little while because they had to check my identity before they could even talk to me about another guest at the hotel. I explained that I was meant to be looking after her, so eventually they must have seen by the way I spoke, slightly agitated and almost losing my patience, that I was serious. They agreed to phone her room. But, of course, there was no answer, I could have told them that. And then I was thinking what kind of way was this to look after her? I should never have let her out of my sight.

What was I thinking, letting a child go up in the elevator alone?

One of the staff at the reception agreed to go up with me in order to check. And the trip in the elevator is longer than you think. There was nothing to say, no point in trying to get friendly with this man or trying to gain his trust and win him over by making some remark about the weather. He wanted to retain his doubts about me. He was not going to be drawn in until he got this clarified. So the elevator moved almost without moving. I was thinking about the dial reaching the fourth floor. The doors opened and the man from the reception walked at normal pace ahead of me, no hurry. He knocked on the door, politely calling out her name. All of which takes time. Valuable seconds spent on formalities before he eventually looked at me and looked at the door and then put his hand up to indicate that I should stand back, while he took the initiative and made the decision to open the door. He stepped into the room, cautiously at first, coughing and calling her name, you never know what you might come across in a situation like that. And she was not there. I knew it. I ran past him to check the bathroom, but there was no sign of her there either.

She was lost in the hotel somewhere, but where?

The man called the reception to report a guest missing, in a wheelchair. He gave her name and the room number. It was all about procedure and what to do next. But I had no time to wait. I went back down again, trying to work out what had happened. She must have been unable to find her room, just as I had suspected. The only thing to do now was to search for her, floor by floor, and then I heard her voice.

Inside the elevator, I heard her calling. She was not in the elevator, but I could hear her voice clearly calling me.

Liam. Liam. That's all I heard.

I couldn't work out where. I called back. Other guests arriving with suitcases may have found it a bit unsettling, to see me coming out of the elevator calling, looking around as if I was lost, not right. I went up another floor and her voice was not there any more, so back down I went again until I could hear her, we were in communication. I thought she was in the elevator shaft somewhere. Incarcerated, inside the wall, or in the stairwell. Or maybe in some kind of storage area. I couldn't figure it out. And then eventually I narrowed it down to the basement, she had to be down there, that was the only thing left I could think of. Why did it take me so long to work that out?

The way I explained it to myself is that she went down in the one elevator that led to the basement, where I had not been looking. The other two elevators don't go down that far. That was the problem. She had got the elevator that leads down to the underground car park.

When I found her she was very upset. She was frightened and confused, breathing very rapidly, not making sense. The card key for the room was still in her hand, held tightly. She would not let it go. She was looking around to get her bearings, no idea where she was. And the surroundings were not like upstairs, no hardwood panelling or soft carpets. It was cold down there, with bare, bright lights and no need for décor, only scuffed paintwork. All this time, while I was trying to find out if she was in her room, she was trapped in the basement, shivering.

Liam, she said. I saw my brother.

I tried to calm her down.

I saw him, she said. Jimmy.

I tried to take her hand but she pulled away from me. She must have thought I was not going to believe what she was saying, because she kept repeating that she saw her brother. She said she tried to call the elevator and then she saw her little brother, he was whispering to her, she didn't know what he was saying.

He was looking into my eyes, she said. He's in trouble, Liam, he needs me.

Maybe it was all the medication. She was shivering and not getting enough air. And she was complaining of a horrible taste in her mouth, like chalk. Chalk and custard and bits of tobacco leaves, bits of seaweed, she said, stuck at the back of her throat. I gave her the see-through bag in case she wanted her medication, something to calm her down and bring her back to herself, maybe a bit of chocolate to get the taste of custard and seaweed out of her mouth. And then I did the breathing song with her. I told her to relax and breathe in and out calmly. Because it sounded like she had been in a race, completely out of breath, her nose was running. When you're ready, I said, take in a deep breath and hold it for as long as you can, very good, hold it, hold it. Then I told her to let it all the way out again, all the way, all the way, all the way, very good, but she could only manage a few shallow puffs. I wanted her to try it again, one more time, but she was too upset. She was hardly getting any air at all into her lungs. As if time was running out. She was searching all around to see where her brother was, asking me if I could see him, would I go and check in those little rooms, those closets where he might be hiding, all the storage places where they keep detergents and cream cleansers and bath mats and shower caps and toilet rolls, all those little shampoo bottles people take with them and which have to be replaced for each new guest, because she worked in room service once and she would know where all these things were kept. Was he in any of those places hiding, she said, maybe in one of the empty boxes of materials delivered to the hotel, behind a trolley that was loaded with spare pillows and duvets and bedspreads, hiding to get away from the noise in his head of what he remembered as a child? Was he in the place where they do the washing, behind the dryers rotating, in the room where they store all the linen, was he in one of those presses stacked up with fresh linen, to keep safe?

I had to get her out of the basement as quickly as possible. Come on, I said to her, let's go back upstairs. I called the elevator and brought her up to her room, though she was still worried about her brother, saying he was lost and she couldn't leave him down there. So I told her we had to find some way of getting her warm first, then we could go back and look for him. I had to get her into the bath. I had to stop her shivering. I had to get her ready for the opera. I had to pick up the tickets for *Don Carlo*.

46

We left the Adlon Hotel with plenty of time. She was going to see her family. She was going to meet them for the last time, alive on the stage, her father and mother. Her brother. Her family waiting at the Berlin State Opera.

We passed by the Russian Embassy along the way. All the stuff that went on in there, she said, beyond those railings, and the guards so stern and silent outside. Sentry, she said. We passed by souvenir shops with lots of postcards and Berlin guides. Tankards and T-shirts with the green man walking. All the landmarks you could not mistake for any other city, a miniature plastic Brandenburg Gate that people bring home as proof. We continued on Unter den Linden until we got to the university, a big open square where we stopped for a while to look down at the white empty shelves underground. And because she said nothing, because she didn't say go back now, let's not go any further, I pushed the wheelchair on again, out of the square and up towards the entrance of the State Opera with its façade lit up.

Don Carlo.

I pushed her all the way in through the doors, right into the crowd of people waiting in the foyer, people standing in a line to hand in their coats. The smooth silent wheels of the wheelchair running along the carpet. I got her a programme and handed her the red glasses. She had no need for the programme, but she loved holding it in her hands and hearing the voices around her, the buzz, you could feel it.

The ushers were calling out in German and in English, asking people to begin taking their seats. The foyer had chandeliers and gold-painted beading around the walls, like a palace. People were dressed up in their best gear, so to speak, their opera costumes. Women with off-the-shoulder dresses. Men wearing really good suits. Only one thin man in the middle of the crowd dressed in a crumpled jacket and a faded pink T-shirt. He was not interested in style. He was staring into the distance as though he could only concentrate on the opera ahead, like he didn't eat very much and lived only through music, a human ear in the shape of a man.

As we went in to take our seats she was smiling, like she was home at last. The usher took the wheelchair and said he would bring it back in at the interval, it was going to be right outside the door, just so we knew. The place was packed out, including all the private boxes. She looked at the circular dome above and the chandeliers. And then came the moment she was waiting for, when all the voices of people talking at once come together with the instruments tuning up, a million words mixed up with the random sounds of the orchestra, everyone for themselves and no order to it, only a big blur of notes and words before the lights go down and the silence returns and the performance begins.

Can I silence the love within me?

She reminded me of what happens in the opera.

Can I silence that love? The key moment to watch out for, she said, as if she was saying it to herself.

I wondered why Don Carlos doesn't run away, that's what I would have done. It's the first thing that would occur to me, running away. Doesn't everybody do that? Don't we all run away? But I'm not Don Carlos and it's not possible to escape from love. Because Don Carlos is in love with the Queen, the woman his father stole from him. So he can't leave. No more than any one of us can leave. He's trapped inside his life. All the people on stage are trapped in their lives, trapped inside the family. They can't run away because their lives will come after them.

And then something quite strange happened on stage. As the story begins to unfold and the King decides to kill the love inside himself to uphold his reign, he begins ruthlessly exercising his power and all these naked captives appear on stage, tied up with ropes around their wrists and feet. They are in very bad shape, tortured and starved, with lash marks across their bodies. I remembered walking by the sea once with my mother on a stormy day in the summer and we saw a man like that with cuts all over his body, like a crucifix, my mother said.

259

He had been thrown without mercy against the rocks by the waves. He was shivering, I remember. Under his shoulder, the skin had been torn right off, like a piece missing, his knees were red and his towel was pink with blood and he was just staring back at the waves that nearly killed him. That's what the King in *Don Carlo* had ordered his men to do to these people on stage, make them look like male and female people on the cross.

While the King is having dinner with his family, his son stands up and threatens his father with a knife. There is a struggle and the knife is taken from Don Carlos. Then everything carries on as planned and the half-crucified people get strung up. Men in black paramilitary gear come in and pour petrol all over them. The naked and lashed people are left hanging by their feet, upside-down, above the stage, covered in petrol. I'm serious. All these half-alive men and women suspended by ropes around their ankles over the stage, blood and petrol dripping from their bodies and their hair falling down, they look like carcasses. While the King continues having his dinner and drinking wine, the Queen has to sit there and keep him company, even though she doesn't love him, she loves his son instead, Don Carlos.

What is that for? Úna said. What are all those poor people doing naked on stage?

They're the victims, so I gather. People who spoke against the King.

That is ridiculous, she said.

She actually laughed out loud. More like a laugh and a shout together. What? Because she had seen this particular opera many times and she had never seen anything like this before. Never, she said. They had nothing like this at the Met. Have they no imagination left? Does everything barbaric have to be so barbaric on the stage, she said.

It is a bit barbaric, I agreed.

This is terrible, Liam. This whole thing is wrong.

She was getting quite worked up. Rubbish, she was saying, which I believe she was quite entitled to do, responding emotionally to the drama. People were shouting bravo every now and then to make sure they could be heard listening. So what was wrong with her offering her opinion as well.

This is awful, she shouted. Awful. Awful. Awful.

I asked her to keep her voice down but she couldn't. Her imagination was too big. She didn't have her bag with her either, so there was no medication at hand to calm her down.

Please, one of the men close to us said.

And then luckily the interval came. The men in paramilitary gear came to set fire to the naked people. So I ran and got the wheelchair. She was still shouting on the way out, saying it was wrong not to allow us to imagine the worst for ourselves. But then I knew it was not the naked people that were bothering her so much as her own brother up on stage. Her own family in front of her eyes.

She didn't want to go back after the interval. We were waiting in the foyer and once the audience began to take their seats again for the second part of the evening, she put her hand up to let me know that she wanted to stay out.

I don't want to see my brother like this, she said.
So we didn't take our seats again. We stayed in the foyer watching all the people drifting back inside. The orchestra started to tune up again without us. We had the foyer to ourselves, except for one of the ushers coming to ask us if we were waiting for a taxi. She didn't want to stay and she didn't want to leave. She wanted to remain close by and listen without seeing, particularly the aria where the King sings about the Queen having no love for him.

I was curious to find out what happens in the end, how the father kills his own son. I asked her how Don Carlos dies, but she seemed to forget which family I was talking about. She said he came back to Dublin and he could never find his feet again. She said she bought an apartment for him to live in but that didn't mean all that much to him and he was not really able to live on his own. She couldn't give him any more money because she thought he would only kill himself with it, that's how she put it. I didn't want to kill him with money. He was taking all kinds of drugs and drinking heavily and nobody could rescue him. She was in New York at the time and she kept asking to find out how he was, but it was hard to come back and see him going downhill, not even feeding himself, only drinking and hiding to forget. And then he was found one day lying out in the back garden, face down like his own mother.

She said it was not her father who killed him. Her father and mother were in love, and maybe that's the danger of people being so insanely in love, they

262

didn't care about their children. Her brother was a casualty of love, she said.

Instead of continuing to accuse her father of murder, this time she was pointing the finger at herself. I think it was hard for her to say this. She said she should have looked out for her brother a bit more, she could have rescued him.

I cannot forgive myself, she said.

After the interval, in the foyer, she said this to me. She spoke in a quiet voice, still listening to the music, possibly made aware of something by the music that she had not allowed herself to say before. I cannot forgive myself, she said, for letting my brother down. For not allowing him to look into my eyes, back in London, when he needed me. He was the youngest, you know, and I should have cared for him. I should have been his mother for him. I should have been his father for him. Instead of sending him off into the world on his own.

You did what you could.

It was me who killed him, she said.

No you didn't, don't say that.

I could have saved him, Liam. It was up to me, nobody else. Once I knew he was abandoned by his own father and mother, he was in my care, nobody's responsibility but mine. What use is happiness if you leave your brother behind? What does it matter, my artistic life, my rage, my books and all the public attention I got? Was he the price of my success? His happiness the price of mine? Because I knew he was not able to live on his own, without help. He was nobody without me. He was in trouble from the beginning and I did nothing, she said. I was not ready to give up on myself and give away that glimmer of talent, the little tricks I pulled with words, those things that impressed people, the little collection of stories I kept in my head to describe my life. I was afraid to sacrifice that right to be myself in order to keep my brother from going down. I loved him but I was not able to do that, Liam, I could not give up my life for his.

She continued listening to the music.

I should have brought him with me, she said. I should have gone travelling with him.

The music was lifting her words as she began talking about all the places in the world she never got to see because she had not thought of bringing her brother with her. If only I had not abandoned him. He would have given me the courage to go places I had only dreamed of before.

I should have dropped everything, she said. I should not have been so worried about my independence and wanting to create something for myself. Sure what have I got in the end, he's my story, my reflection, my weakness. I should have been his big sister, his friend, his travelling companion. I should have said to him, listen, Jimmy, we are going to go travelling together. You and me. Come on, Jimmy, I should have said, let's go away.

Anywhere away.

If only I could go back, she said, I would bring him with me this time. That's what I would do in my next life. If there was such a thing as the next life, I would take him with me and never let him out of my sight. Jimmy, are you ready, I would say to him. The tickets are booked. We would live like it was the only life. We would start in Berlin and then we would go on trains all across Europe. And when we were finished with Europe, we would move on to Asia and Latin America, all down through South America we would travel together. I would give up writing books and speaking in public. I would stop talking about my life and my family, my memory. We would remember nothing about where we came from and what happened back home, we would keep on travelling, just the two of us, me and my brother Jimmy.

It said in the death notice that she was with her brother now.

Sure what does it matter that he was drinking, she said.

On the gravestone, they have the name of her brother and her own name underneath.

Sure what does it matter that he was taking drugs.

Only the two names together, along with the dates of birth and the dates they died.

We could have had the time of our lives, she said, travelling up and down the world, across the equator how many times, round as often as we liked, all down to the Galápagos and the Indian Ocean and Sri Lanka and Tibet, all those parts of the world in whatever order they come, places that I don't know yet, all the people we would meet and all the packed trains and suitcases and people sleeping where suitcases are supposed to be kept, back over to Africa where life started in the first place and God knows

265

where do you go on to from there, she said, to the ends of the earth. I should have gone to the ends of the earth for him.

Sure what does it matter as long as we were travelling, she said. What does it matter only that we kept on travelling.

47

The shoes. The red canvas shoes. I keep thinking that if I had them, I would have brought them back to Berlin with me. That's the place for them, I feel. I'm only imagining this now. If I had her shoes, I would take them with me in my bag, I would be looking for some place that would keep them long-term. Of course, I don't know where the shoes are, sneakers, Converse, whatever they're called now, with the white rubber soles and the rough white stitching and the little steel eyelets for the laces and one lace broken. If it was up to me, if I was in charge of her shoes, I would be storing them somewhere around the city, but where? I'm thinking of the *U-Bahn*, I would love to put them on top of one of the yellow trains. I would tie the shoelaces together to stop them from getting separated. They would travel back and forth forever underneath the city, indefinitely. But these trains get cleaned regularly, don't forget, so the shoes might disappear and never be seen again. Better still. If I had them, her shoes, I might even take them with me to the Pergamon

Museum, into the room with all those bits of marble that don't fit together any more, unfinished. There's a pillar I've been looking at, medium height, where I could easily throw them up on top. They would be there forever, part of this permanent exhibition of Greek artefacts. But it's only a thought, of course, never to be carried out. Maybe the rightful thing to do with her shoes would be to bring them back to Clare, that's where they belong. Where her shoes covered most ground. Maybe they should be brought back to the Burren, somewhere out along the cliffs. On a ledge somewhere, out of reach. But I don't have them. The shoes. The red canvas shoes. I have no idea where they are.

48

I'm going through the photographs of Berlin and there is one I have of her at the memorial. She is surrounded by all those grey columns. It shows her from the side, sitting in her wheelchair, shoulders hunched against the wind. Her hand is holding the collar of her black coat around her neck. She looks cold. Her head is bowed, uncovered, no hair. She's staring at the ground. And it's not one of those photographs like so many of the others where she's doing her best to smile at the camera.

She has taken off her cap. Why? I don't know.

It's a hard photograph to look at, with her head bare and nothing but grey columns around her, some that are not straight either, leaning to one side, uneven, sinking columns.

I think it was a hard place for her to go to. Because she was dying and still she wanted to remember millions of other people dead. It was hard for her, I think, to say to herself that she was less important than all those other people. She felt small and insignificant, so she told me afterwards.

As though her death was not really much to speak about now. Not even the death of her own brother could matter here. There was something about sitting among the grey columns that haunted her. As though she was in a church with no roof and no windows and you were not really meant to speak.

I suppose it's such an instinctive thing, taking a photograph. I get the camera out of my pocket, I don't know why. I suppose I'm trying to keep something, trying to hold on to her. In fact, it's only when I step back to take the photograph that she takes off the cap. She holds the collar of her coat around her neck with one hand and takes her cap off with the other. I don't really know why she has made the decision to take off the cap at this moment, in the cold. This is the time to put on your cap, not the time to take it off. But maybe it's something she does out of respect. It looks like her head has been shaved. Her skull is exposed to the wind. She looks like she's closer to death than ever before. She cannot get any closer to death. But she is still alive in that photograph. And there is still time in that photograph to push the wheelchair away, there is still time to get back to the car and back to the hotel, there's still time for her to see her family, there's still time to get her back to Dublin before she is dead.

I know she must be freezing by now. We have been there for a long time and she has said nothing about being cold. I have no idea that she is shivering, not until I get her back to the car and Manfred says it. After he lifts her back in and he turns around to me, folding up the wheelchair.

Your mother is shivering, he says.

So we get her back to the hotel as quickly as possible. We don't have far to go, only around the corner. We could easily walk it, but it's too late and she's too cold and this is not the time to take our time. And when she gets back to the Adlon, she says she'll be fine. I tell her that she's shivering but she denies it. And then of course she goes missing and when I find her at last in the basement of the hotel, she is definitely shivering.

The only thing for me to do is to give her a bath. I have to get her warm again. I have to get the life back into her. I get her up to the room and run the water and it comes gushing out very fast. Big brass taps. And a lovely heavy stopper on a chain. It's a very spacious bath and the bathroom is full of steam, there's a nice echo around the tiles of water flowing into water.

Her hands are cold and I have to rub them to try and get the heat back into them. I take each one of her hands into my hands and rub as fast as I can. I rub her wrists as though I'm putting a shine on them with the heel of my hand. Then I do the same with the feet. I get the shoes off, the red canvas shoes which are absolutely no use for the cold, even with socks on. They're only good for the summer. I start rubbing her feet and the ankles, with both of my hands moving like a machine to get the circulation going.

I'm running around preparing the towels, very

271

large, thick towels, laying them out on a chair. I put
all the bath salts available into the bath and almost
half a bottle of the amber stuff that makes the whole
bath bubble up so you can hardly see the clear green
water underneath. I don't know how much is
enough. Nothing is enough and I add a drop of the
other jade bottle as well. So the scent around the
bathroom is comforting, the lighting is soft and
maybe that will begin to get her back to herself again.

You'll soon be warm again, I tell her.

She can't speak. She seems to have no feeling at
all. She's not even conscious of me removing her
clothes and her eyes are glazed over, hardly even
aware that she's in a hotel bathroom with the bath
filling up right next to her and the foam rising.

Her arms are gone floppy. It's easy to lift them
and take her blue jumper off, but I have to make
sure not to drop her arms each time, they have no
energy in them to stay up by themselves. It takes a
while for me to get the bra undone and she doesn't
help. I slip her clothes off and place them on a chair.
I switch off the water and test it with my hand and
add a bit more cold, then I test it again with my
elbow, the way you do for a baby.

I've completely overdone it with the foam.

I place her arms around me to lift her up out of
the wheelchair. I manage to lift one leg up over the
rim of the bath and into the water, then the other,
so she's standing in the bath and I'm holding on to
her. I let her sink down slowly and the temperature
seems just right. Only when she's sitting down in
the warm water and her senses are slowly coming

back to her, then she can finally begin to speak again.

Thanks, Liam, she says.

She's sitting forward with her knees up and her arms around her knees. The foam comes all the way up around her neck, right over the rim of the bath, separating into lumps and falling out on the floor. I can hear the foam crackling, balls of it sticking to my arms.

And then her body gives a big shake. As though she's got a fright. Her body shudders with all that sudden warmth around her. Her mouth makes a sound, something she can't stop herself saying, only it's not a word, just the sound of her calling out. Like she's shivering in reverse now, shivering with the heat. Shivering with the life coming back into her. Because it's quite a shock, going from such a cold place with all those grey columns to such a warm place inside the hotel bathroom.

I dip the face-cloth into the water with all the soap and I lay it out across her back. Her skin is very smooth, very soft to touch. I can feel her breathing under my hand. She is leaning forward with her hands up to her face and I rub the cloth very lightly around in circles.

It's all right, I tell her.

Because I know she's crying. I can feel it in her back, the movement in her body. I can't see her face, but I know from the quiet rhythm in her back that she is crying and all I can do is keep rubbing the cloth around and around in circles, telling her it's OK.

Everything is fine now, don't worry.

She's only crying because she's getting warm. She's beginning to feel her own pulse and her own blood moving. The life is coming back into her, that's why she's crying. She's crying because she's alive and she's feeling better now, back to herself again. She is crying for the cold and the warm. She is crying for all the cold and all the warm and all the cold again.

49

There I am on the train, going east. I would love to
have been able to tell her about this. I wish I could
have told her about continuing the journey, beyond
Berlin. I made a stop along the way, near the Polish
border. A photographer invited me to visit a farm
where he has set up a camera that you can walk
into. A box camera, if you like, only life-size. It's
nothing more than a room or a shed made out of
salvaged wood, no windows. It's lined from the
inside with blackout material, every bit of daylight
is blocked out except for one tiny pinhole of light
coming in. Even the door is covered with heavy
black curtains so that when you walk in you're in
complete darkness. You can't even see your own
hand in front of you. I could hear children giggling
right behind me. It turned out they were sitting on
the floor and they could see me stumbling around
like a blind man. It took a while for me to get accustomed to the dark, and the light. Until the room
slowly became brighter and I could see everything
turned upside-down on the walls. That's what they

had all come to see. Everything gets turned upside-down, I knew that from school, but I had never actually seen it for myself. The sky and the clouds were down close to the floor. And up near the ceiling, a line of upside-down trees and houses with red roofs. Then I saw the children and their mothers sitting around me, while their fathers were outside, jumping upside-down with their arms in the air, falling out of the sky. That was it, I stayed there for a while inside the box camera, looking at the world on its head, then I left and got back on the train.

Many thanks to Peter Straus, Nicholas Pearson, Olly Rowse, Robert Lacey, Colm Tóibín, Daniel Arsand, Vera Michalski-Hoffmann, Petra Eggers, Georg Reuchlein, Charles A. Heimbold, Joseph Lennon, John and Kathy Immerwahr, and especially to Mary (Boyce) Doorly (Limerick/Ottawa – February 2012) who gave me the title *Every Single Minute*.